MW00533575

TWISTED CHRONICLES

TWISTED CHRONICLES

TRUDY-ANN CAMPBELL

Charleston, SC
www.PalmettoPublishing.com

Twisted Chronicles

First Edition

Hardcover ISBN: 978-1-68515-238-3
Paperback ISBN: 978-1-68515-239-0
eBook ISBN: 978-1-68515-240-6

Contents

The Killer

Laughter, chatter, and the smell of pumpkin spice coffee filled the air of the office building of Ruben Charles. It was 9:30 a.m., business as usual. Ruben's employees buzzed like worker bees, trying to get their busy day going. But all that came to a halt when James Caviler walked into Ruben's office and found him on the floor, lying in a pool of his own blood. Mr. Charles was murdered, with his throat slashed from ear to ear, blood on the walls, papers scattered, and desk drawers left open. James stood in the doorway, frozen in horror, before letting out a bloodcurdling scream, which could be heard throughout the entire office building.

"He's dead! He's dead! Someone please call 911!"

Panic spread throughout the building like wildfire. But who would want to kill Ruben Charles, such a wealthy and well-liked member of society, right before Christmas? Ruben Charles could have any woman or man hypnotized with his ravishing and mesmerizing good looks. One gaze into his big brown eyes would leave you spellbound and wondering what just happened. Ruben was a well-known CEO of one of the largest law firms in the country. He was also said to be a high roller in the casino world.

Sobbing and whispering employees of Ruben Charles watched on in shock and disbelief as the coroner hauled off his lifeless body. They couldn't come to terms with what they were witnessing. No one was allowed to leave the building until they were thoroughly questioned by the FBI. They set up shop, and one by one, the employees were interrogated. The FBI wanted to make sure they got everyone's version of the event while it was still fresh in their memories and any clues that might be useful in solving the case. The questioning went on for what seemed like hours.

There were several theories floating around about who might have wanted Mr. Charles dead—a betrayed wife, angry clients, mistresses, or someone he owed money to from one of his many poker games. Most of the theories didn't even make sense, but one thing was prevalent about everyone's recollections of the days leading up to the murder—James and Ruben were frequently heard having heated conversations. About what, no one could really say. Without any other leads or suspects, James quickly found himself at the top of the FBI's list as their prime suspect.

After all the employees were questioned and sent home, the FBI began combing through the entire office building, trying to find a motive for the murder, but what they found next would send the case in a tailspin. They found a receipt for a gas station almost two thousand miles away. Now the unanswered question was. What was Ruben Charles doing so far away from home? Following the paper trail, the FBI ended up in a small town in Texas called Orla. Suddenly, the mistress theory seemed far-fetched but probable. It was hard to believe that Ruben Charles was a cheater because he was often seen in public treating his wife with the utmost respect. He worshipped the very ground she walked on, and in her eyes he could do no wrong.

While the FBI was on their wild goose chase, James was brought in by the local police department for a second round of questioning. While in the interrogation room, James wasn't even offered a bottle of water; the officers just got right to the point.

"So, Mr. Caviler, what were you and Mr. Charles arguing about in the days leading up to his death?" the officer asked.

"We were not arguing," James replied in a snotty tone.

"OK, let me rephrase the question. What were you and Mr. Charles talking about so very intensely?" the officer asked again.

"We were having a private conversation. Is that a crime?" James was so matter-of-fact with his answers, which wasn't working in his favor.

The officers grew more and more irritated as the interrogation went on. One of the officers glanced at the camera over his left shoulder. Pushing his chair back, he stood aggressively, slammed both palms down on the cold, hard stainless steel table that separated himself from James, and said to him in a very stern voice, "Let me be clear. Unless you want to go to jail for his murder, I suggest you come clean right now."

James flinched and straightened up in his chair. Suddenly, he wasn't feeling so comfortable anymore.

"We were discussing business proposition. I swear I had nothing to do with his death. I still can't believe he's gone," James replied.

"So is this business so top secret that you can't enlighten us with the details of the conversation?" the officer asked sarcastically.

With a roll of the eyes, James replied, "No, it's not, sir."

The officer quickly realized that his bad cop approach is rendering ineffective and tried to change up his tactics a bit.

"Look, James, you have to give us something we can use to clear your name, or else you'll leave us no choice but to charge you for the murder until it can be proven otherwise."

What the officer said to James must have snapped him back to reality because the moment he heard *charge* and *murder* in the same sentence, he started singing like a canary.

"OK, here's the thing. I wanted to start my own law firm, and let's just say Mr. Charles wasn't ready for our partnership to end, if you know what I mean." With a flirty smile on his face, James stared dead straight at the officers.

James was Ruben Charles's assistant and right-hand man, but not only that; he was also accused of making sexual passes at Ruben several weeks ago.

"Are we done here?" James asked.

"For your sake, let's hope your story checks out. And, James, don't leave town," the officer replied.

James got up and walked out of the interrogation room a freeman, for the moment at least.

* * *

Back in Orla, Texas, the FBI thought they hit a dead end when the gas station clerk couldn't identify a picture of Ruben and hadn't noticed his car being there. That was until Det. Daniel Truman spotted a surveillance camera on a building across the street. Detective Truman and his partner, Detective Walker, made their way over to the antique store, trying their very best to avoid the busy traffic of two passing cars. Truman pulled open the door to the antique store, which set off an old-timey chime. There stood behind the counter the store owner, Lavinia. She was a stunningly gorgeous gypsy woman, who was wearing a yellow sundress with tiny red birds on it. She had the most beautiful jet-black hair you'd ever seen, which was pulled up into a high ponytail, and she wore a bright red lipstick on her small lips. She had a welcoming smile and honest eyes tucked away behind her red framed glasses.

"Hello and welcome to Halo's Find. Can I help you, gentlemen, find anything in particular?" Lavinia asked cheerfully.

"Hi, I'm Detective Truman, and this is my partner, Detective Walker. We are working a case and would really appreciate your help," Truman said, introducing himself as he flashed his shiny FBI badge.

"I don't know how I can be of any help to your case, Detectives," she replied.

"I see you have a surveillance camera on the outside of your building, which is facing the gas station across the street." Detective Truman pointed to the gas station. "Do you mind if I take a look?" he asked.

Lavinia agreed. "Sure, but I don't know how clear the footage really is."

Truman stepped behind the counter, popped the disc in, pressed play, and prayed he would find something, anything that might shed some light on the case. The footage was rolling, but there was no sign of Ruben Charles, just people making their routine gas station stop. About five minutes into the footage, Detective Walker was ready to call it quits, but that was when Ruben's black Aston Martin pulled into the gas station. He stepped out of his car and proceeded to fill up his gas tank, but right before he left, a silver Dodge Charger with heavily tinted windows pulled up next to him. A Caucasian male emerged from the driver's side, wearing a T-shirt, blue jeans, and a base-ball cap. Ruben Charles handed off very discreetly a large brown envelope. Detective Truman took a long, hard look at the man receiving the envelope. Even though he wore a baseball cap, his features were recognizable. He had a familiar face, but it couldn't be. He was a fellow detective. It was Det. Ryan Wall. A look of confusion washed over Truman's face.

"May I keep the footage?" Detective Truman asked the store owner.

"Yes, if it will help your case, you go right ahead," she replied.

Detective Truman left the antique store with a sickening feeling in the pit of his stomach.

* * *

Back at the FBI headquarters, Truman was at his desk with his hands covering his face, a million and one questions swirling around in his head. *Why was Detective Wall meeting Ruben Charles? Is Detective Wall working on the case? What's in the envelope? What does his wife know about any of this? Of course, the wife! Why didn't I think about her?* A light bulb must have gone off in Truman's head that sent him leaping out of his seat. He grabbed his jacket off the back of his chair and his keys and badge off his desk and headed over to Ruben's house to find out if his wife had any knowledge of what Ruben might have been working on before he was murdered.

Detective Truman pulled up to the Charleses' residence in a whoosh. With no time to lose, he hopped out of his Range Rover and strode eagerly up the spacious walkway lined with beautifully manicured, ready-to-bloom multicolored roses on either side. He knocked on the enormous blue door. Agonizing moments later, the door opened, and an old butler materialized on the other side. Truman flashed his badge.

"One moment please," the butler said.

He closed the door in Truman's face and retreated into the elaborate mansion. A few minutes later, the door opened again, and this time it was Ruben's wife, Elizabeth. She had legs for days wrapped up in a skintight burgundy leather pants with stilettos, as if her legs weren't long enough. Truman's eyes traveled slowly up her perfect body, passing her voluptuous breasts to reveal her full lips, gorgeous red mane, and cerulean eyes. Truman almost forgot why he was there in the first place.

"May I help you?" Elizabeth asked with such grief in her voice.

"Hi, Mrs. Charles…"

"Elizabeth," she corrected him.

"My name is Detective Truman," he said, with a show of his badge and an outstretched arm. "I'm here to do a follow-up on your husband's case," Detective Truman stated.

Elizabeth just stared at him with her arms still folded, making no effort to entertain a handshake. Truman slowly rippled his fingers and returned his hand to his pocket.

The FBI, Elizabeth thought. "What does the FBI want with my husband's case?" she heard herself asking.

"Well, Mrs. Charles...Elizabeth, your husband owns the country's leading law firm, and given the circumstances of his untimely death, his case is considered high profile so the FBI was called in to treat it as such," Truman quickly clarified.

"So why are you here and not out there trying to find who killed my husband?" she asked angrily.

"I was wondering if you could answer a few questions for me."

"I already told that other detective all I knew, which isn't much. My husband is...was a very private man," Elizabeth stated.

"Just answer what you can," he said.

And with that, Elizabeth showed him inside the mansion. They proceeded into the living room and over to the luxurious white couches, where they sat opposite each other. The butler brought coffee and sat it on a glass table in between them.

"OK, Detective, what would you like to know?" she questioned.

"Do you know a Det. Ryan Wall?" Truman asked.

"No. Why? Should I know him? Did he have something to do with my husband's death?" Elizabeth asked, answering the question with questions of her own that went unanswered by the detective.

"Do you know anything about the last case your husband might have been working on?" Truman asked a different question.

"No. Like I said earlier, Detective, my husband was a very private man. He didn't share the details of his cases with me," she replied, following it up with a question of her own. "What does Det. Ryan Wall have to do with my husband's case?"

Detective Truman proceeded to take notes, trying to avoid giving an answer. Truman quickly shut down any further questions from Elizabeth by saying, "It's an ongoing case, and therefore, I'm not at liberty to share the details with you. I'm sorry."

Elizabeth stood straight away and said, "If you are not at liberty to share, then I think we are done here."

With her right hand as straight as an arrow, she gestured to the door. Detective Truman then got up and showed himself out the way he came in.

"I'm so sorry for your loss, Mrs. Charles," he said before he exited.

Elizabeth replied, "If you're so sorry, Detective, you'll find who did this to my Ruben."

With tears streaming down her face, she closed the door before Truman could say, "Have a nice day, ma'am." But he said it anyways. With no useful information from Elizabeth Charles, Detective Truman departed for his office.

* * *

The next day, Elizabeth received a package containing a large brown envelope. Inside the envelope there were files with numerous transactions, offshore bank accounts and other numerical figures that Elizabeth has no comprehension of, and a note that reads, "Trust no one!"

Elizabeth was putting the envelope and its contents on the marble kitchen counter when out fell a flash drive. Perplexed, she twirled the flash drive on the kitchen counter with her finger, attempting to make sense of it all to no avail. She made the decision not to check what was on the flash drive at that moment. She figured the less she knew, the safer she would be. "But there must be someone I can trust," she reassured herself.

* * *

With no new leads, it was back to the drawing broad for Detective Truman. But there was one lead the detective hadn't explored yet. With the burden of expectations weighing heavily on his shoulders and his reputation on the line, Detective Truman reluctantly picked up the phone to call Det. Ryan Wall, who headed the undercover unit. He was very cocky at times and was said to be Truman's rival. Some said they had a healthy competition going on, but Truman would tell them otherwise. Truman couldn't stand the sight of him and would rather stab himself in the ear with a pencil than have to hear Detective Wall's voice. Truman didn't stab himself in the ear; he just put on his big boy pants and dialed the number.

"Hello, Detective Wall. Detective Truman here."

"What can I do for you, Detective?" Wall asked.

"I'm working on a case, and I think you can help."

"Sure thing, Detective, anything you need." With superiority overtaking Wall, he was more than eager to help.

"I think we should meet later today and go over the details," Truman said.

"We can do it over the phone. These lines are secure," Wall pointed out.

"It's best if we meet in person," Truman insisted.

"OK, just email me the location," Wall replied, giving in to Truman's demands.

"Sending it to you right…now. Done."

"All right, see you at round 7:30 p.m.," Wall said.

When 7:30 p.m. rolled around, they met up at the local bikers' bar, on S23 and Fifth Hoverton Street While there; they ordered a few rounds of beer and exchanged work-related stories, trying to surpass each other in the process. Detective Wall was taking a sip of his beer when he remembered why he was actually there.

"Hmm, what is it you wanted to know?" Wall asked, almost spilling his drink.

"I'm working on the Charles case," Truman replied.

"Oh yeah, I heard about that. So tragic," Wall sympathized.

"Tell me about it," Truman said, taking a sip of his beer. "So I have a surveillance tape in my car that I think you should take a look at. I think maybe you can help me put the pieces together."

"Yeah, why's that?" Wall asked.

"Let's just go take a look," Truman urged.

"Can I not finish my beer first?" Wall asked jokingly.

"I want to get this over with," Truman said.

"OK, if you insist."

Wall took one last sip of his beer, and they both got up to leave. Detective Wall pulled out his wallet and placed a twenty-dollar bill on the counter as they headed out. Truman suspiciously eyed the crowd from left to right while trailing behind Detective Wall as they exited the bar. They crossed the street and came upon Truman's parked car under a streetlamp. Detective Truman looked around, taking notice. They must have been in the bar for about an hour because dusk has fallen on the lively street corner of S23 and Fifth. They both entered the front of the car and Truman popped open his laptop to show the surveillance footage to Detective Wall.

"Yep, that's definitely me," Wall stated.

"Can you enlighten me on the nature of your relationship with Ruben Charles and the reason for the meet in Texas?" Truman asked.

Wall replied, "Detective, I really would like to help, but my hands are tied."

"Come on, there must be something you can give me. What's in the envelope Ruben gave you?" Truman pressed him for answers.

"Like I said, my hands are tied, but hey, did you question his wife to see if she might know anything?" Detective Wall asked, offering other options and trying to be of some use to his fellow detective.

"I already did, and she had no fucking clue about what her husband does," Truman replied, showing signs of frustration.

"I understand your frustration. I really do, but I don't know how much more I can help you," Wall said.

Detective Truman was finally out of leads and options at this point, but he wasn't going to give up that easily.

"Come on man," Truman urged, sounding even more desperate than ever.

Wall confessed, "There might be something I can give you."

An elated Truman replied, "Really? I owe you big time!"

Detective Wall wrote down a number. "Call this number and explain the case you're working on. They should be able to help you more than I can."

"Thanks, man," Truman said.

And with that, Wall exited the car.

* * *

Meanwhile, at the Ruben Charles law firm, employees tried to pick up the pieces of what was left and moved on with their new reality. Ruben's office was still under lock and key, given that the case was still ongoing and fresh in everyone's mind. Yellow caution tape sealed the doorway, no one in or out of his office.

With Ruben Charles out of the picture, James Caviler would now have to assume the CEO role. It had always been a lifelong dream of his to be the CEO of his own company. But James would have to take a tantalizing glimpse at the career he had always wanted as it wasn't permanent. James's fellow office mates, or rather his employees, gossiped that James was prancing around as though he was the boss all along and it was his company. They even went as far as to say he would never be Ruben Charles. Word got back to James via a little birdie named Susan, and he was infuriated, lashing out at any and every one of them in his path. Some said he was just angry about the loss of his boss and close friend, while others speculated that he was angry for the simple fact that he wasn't being treated like Ruben Charles.

Ruben's cause of death was already determined by the laceration on his neck. He was damn near decapitated; therefore Elizabeth Charles refused an autopsy. The funeral service was set to be an intimate gathering with family and close friends at the Charleses' residence. Even though that was known to the public, there was no denying the massive turnout, which spoke volumes about his value in society. Even in this intimate setting, people just couldn't help themselves. As Elizabeth consoled Ruben's mom, there were still some speculations, questioning her motive in the marriage. Disgusted by it all, she kindly asked everyone to leave.

* * *

Days later, Elizabeth was having tea and watching her daily program in her living room at home, trying to wrap her mind around her husband's death and the whole anonymous package situation, when it suddenly got interrupted by breaking news. A black news anchor lady in a newsroom setting appeared on the screen.

"Today the city of New York is deeply saddened once again at the loss of one of their own detectives. Det. Daniel Truman was an FBI agent who was known for his stellar and unbeatable record of fifteen cases closed per year," the news anchor reported.

A picture of the detective stood still in the right-hand corner of the screen.

"Detective Truman was found on S23 and Fifth Hoverton Street in his car with a single gunshot wound to his left temple. Detective Truman was pronounced dead at the scene. At this time the police have neither prime suspect nor any motive for this senseless murder. Prior to his death, Detective Truman was working on the case of Ruben Charles, the wealthy CEO of one of the largest law firms in the country who was found murdered in his office building just a few weeks ago. It's not clear whether or not the two cases are connected as of this time. It's still an ongoing case. The city of New York will truly miss their presence. May their souls rest in peace. And with that, we turn to Jim for your updated forecast," she said with sadness in her voice.

Elizabeth was stunned, paralyzed by the breaking news. She was trying to avoid watching the contents of the flash drive, but after hearing of a second murder in such a short period, she had no choice. If these two cases were connected and she couldn't trust the police, who could she turn to for help? Conflicted and burdened by the unfamiliarity of the contents of the package, Elizabeth went against the warning note. She picked up the phone to call the one person whom she thought she could trust. With shaky hands, she dialed the number. The phone rang about four times before a male voice echoed on the other end. With fear in her voice, Elizabeth forced herself to speak.

"Hi, is this James? James Caviler?"

Very hesitantly he answered, "Yes, this is he."

"Hi, this is Elizabeth Charles."

Wide eyed, he replied in a high-pitched voice, "Oh hi, Elizabeth. I am so sorry for your loss. How are you holding up?"

It was the first time they had spoken since the incident.

"Thank you. I'm holding." Very uncertain if she was making the right decision, she managed to get the words out. "I need your help."

James, confused as to why she might need his help, quickly replied, "Sure. Anything."

Right before she told him what it was that she needed his help with, there was a long pause. She was starting to second-guess herself. *Am I doing the right thing by sharing this with him?* she wondered.

"Elizabeth, are you there?" James called out.

Elizabeth snapped out of it, and before she could change her mind, she said, "Yes, I'm here."

"You said you needed my help?" James reminded her.

Elizabeth blurted out in one breath, "Yes, I'm looking at this package here on my kitchen counter, and inside there are a lot of numerical figures, bank account numbers after numbers that I don't understand, a note that says, 'Trust no one,' and a flash drive that I haven't checked yet. I don't know who else to turn to. I think it might have something to do with Ruben's death."

Listening to a very distraught Elizabeth, James couldn't do anything but agree to help her. "Here's what you should do. Put everything up in a safe place until I get there, and, Elizabeth, don't talk to anyone else about this," James said.

Relief overwhelmed her as she slowly returned the phone to its receiver.

James immediately hopped in his red convertible and rushed to the Charleses' residence. He had no idea what he was getting himself into, but all he was thinking about was helping a friend in need.

Elizabeth anxiously awaited his arrival. There was a knock at the door, and without hesitation, Elizabeth opened it, beating the butler to it.

"Come in, come in," she said while ushering James inside.

They made their way into the kitchen, unclear as to what they would do with this newly acquired information. James and Elizabeth sat around the counter, staring blankly at the envelope. There was a deafening silence between the two of them, which was broken by the butler, asking, "Tea, anyone?"

"No, thank you," they both replied in sync.

"Shall we see what's on the flash drive?" James asked.

"Oh, yes, the drive. Let me get my laptop," Elizabeth replied.

Elizabeth returned to the kitchen with her laptop in hand and fear in her eyes. She placed the laptop on the counter, opened it, and turned it on. She plugged the drive, and as she was about to press the enter button, the phone rang, startling them both. They both jumped, nearly falling off their stools. Elizabeth stepped away from the counter to answer the phone, and to her surprise, it was a familiar voice. Before she could say anything, the voice on the other end said, "Don't say anything, and just listen. Trust no one," in a very consequential tone, and then the call ended. Elizabeth gingerly returned the phone to its receiver.

James, watching on, asked, "Is everything OK? You look like you've seen a ghost."

Elizabeth swallowed hard and replied, "Everything's fine, but I think we should do this another time."

"What about the flash drive?" James asked.

"I'm suddenly not feeling well. I really think you should go," Elizabeth explained, holding her head.

"I could take a look at the drive. It won't take long," James said, almost as if he was begging.

"James, I said not now!" Elizabeth shouted.

"OK. Is there anything else I can do for you before I go?" James asked.

"No, I just need to rest a bit," she replied with a weak tone in her voice.

"OK. You have my number. Just call me if you need anything."

"James, thank you for coming." And with that, she showed him out.

Elizabeth closed the door, leaned back on it, and slithered to the ground like a snake, sobbing uncontrollably. She was more confused than ever. She took a few minutes to gather her emotions, and then without hesitation, she darted over to the computer, put the flash drive in, and before she knew it, there was a video playing.

"If you're watching this, that means I am no longer with you. I wish I could tell you what's really going on, but trust me; it's for your own protection. I found out that some really powerful people are doing some really bad things, and when they found out that I was in possession of information that could expose them, they weren't too happy. I didn't know who else to trust with this information, so that's why I gave Det. Ryan Wall a copy and sent one to you too. If you haven't heard about it on the news, it means Det. Ryan Wall buried the information I gave him. So here's what I need you to do. Take the files to the Life Chronicle and ask for a reporter named Dean Deaton. Tell him I sent you. He'll know what to do. And, Elizabeth...be careful. I'm so sorry I'm not there for you, but I promise, *erimus iterum conveniant amica mea,*" Ruben said.

Elizabeth covered her mouth with both hands as tears of joy streamed down her face. She slowly closed the laptop and looked around the room to see if anyone or the butler was looking.

Elizabeth quickly got in her car and headed over to the [Life Chronicle]. It seemed like the longest drive of her life. Elizabeth pulled into the parking lot and ran to the front desk with her oversize handbag containing the files clenched closely to her body.

"Is Dean Deaton here?" she asked the clerk, breathing heavily.

A Goth chick at the front desk peeled her eyes away from the computer screen, held one finger up, picked up the phone, and paged Dean. "Dean Deaton, to the front," blared out over the intercom.

Dean materialized from around a corner. With an outstretched hand, he introduced himself. "Hi, I'm Dean Deaton. And you are?"

"Hi, I'm Elizabeth Charles, and my husband, Ruben Charles, sent me," she replied.

"Yes, yes, of course. Let's go to my office," Dean said reassuringly, and they hurried off to his office. "Come in, sit down," Dean said, showing her to a chair opposite his.

Elizabeth sat, shaking, legs bouncing up and down, and looking all over the place like a scared little child.

"Do you have something for me?" Dean asked.

"Yes," Elizabeth replied quickly. She reached into her handbag and pulled out the files. She ambivalently handed over the files.

Dean took the files and looked them over. Then after about five minutes, he said to Elizabeth, "OK, I'll take it from here. Go home and don't talk to anybody about this. Just watch the news."

Elizabeth left the Life Chronicle with a little sense of relief but still pretty much in fear for her life.

The next day, the news turned the country on its head. Elizabeth turned on the television, and there it was, breaking news. It was all over the television, the internet, and every newspaper.

The news anchor reported, "Today the country must brace itself for the next few days to come. Some disturbing allegations are being brought against the mayor of New York City, Jackie Madison, and the secretary of Homeland Security, Richard Blaze, by an anonymous source. Of course these allegations will undergo a thorough investigation, but with all the paper trail, it doesn't look good for the mayor and the secretary. There are several offshore bank accounts and enormous amounts of wire transfers to a location in Moscow."

The news anchor held a finger to her ear and said enthusiastically, "We are bringing you the updates as they come in. Det. Ryan Wall was also said to be on their payroll. We are getting updates as fast as we can broadcast them. The FBI seemed to have connected the wire transfers in Moscow to a terrorist group that specializes in making biochemical weapons. The mayor and the secretary are being brought in for questioning as we speak." Footage of the mayor and the secretary in police custody materialized on the screen.

Elizabeth turned off the television in shock and disbelief at the revelation that was unfolding right before her very eyes. She had no idea of the magnitude and severity of the cases her husband worked on, day in and day out.

* * *

A month later after the incident, it was a gorgeous Sunday evening. Elizabeth was at a café in downtown Manhattan having tea with her girlfriend Jennifer. She turned her head ever so slightly to look out the glass window in admiration of life. She saw a man across the street staring right at her and had to do a double take, but before she could get a good look at him, an elderly couple stopped in front of the window to share a passionate kiss. She could have sworn she saw Ruben, and instantly a huge smile plastered over her face. Jennifer looked at her suspiciously.

"Elizabeth, are you OK?" she asked.

"I'm OK. In fact I'm better than OK," Elizabeth whispered and smiled with relief.

* * *

While in police custody, the mayor and the secretary quickly turned on each other in hopes of getting a lighter sentence. They both claimed that the other was to be blamed for hatching the plan in the first place, but they both agreed that a domestic terror attack was what the country needed to up its security clearance.

"What's a little collateral damage for the greater good?" the mayor said with such credence.

They were both dragged away in handcuffs to a maximum facility, where they would await trial.

Ut cum in dubio sunt. (When in doubt, get out.)

FIN

The Inheritance

Born on December 25, Christopher Knight was destined for greatness. He was born into wealth and power. While that remained true, he never let that define him or the way he treated people as he was growing up. He was strong willed, independent, and generous. Christopher was the youngest of three kids. He was always in the shadows of his elder siblings—Benjamin, the eldest, and Isabella, the middle child. Benjamin was treated like the golden boy by their father, and Isabella was their mother's princess. Christopher was just Christopher. He never let any of the special treatments his other siblings got corrupt his mind. Christopher was in love with the idea of love, and he loved freely. While the rest of his family turned their noses up at impoverished people and people of color, Christopher embraced them all.

In high school, Christopher took a strong liking to human biology, and sure enough he went on to become a renowned scientist. Isabella became a fashion model. Benjamin stayed at home even after his brother and sister had gone on to make lives of their own, in hopes of inheriting his parents' wealth. After years and years of lying around doing nothing, his parents have had enough. One day they summoned Benjamin to the office to let him know it was time for him to move out, which didn't go over well with him.

"Benjamin, you know your mom and I love you dearly, right?" asked his father.

"Yes, I do, and I love you both dearly. That's why I never left," Benjamin replied jokingly.

"Sure you do," his mom said sarcastically.

"Look, son." His father took a deep breath. "We love having you around, but you don't help out, and so we think it's time for you to go live life outside of these walls, make memories, and have a family of your own," said his dad, Luther, with his wife, Linda, by his side, nodding in agreement.

"But I don't want to do any of that. I just want to stay here with both of you," Benjamin replied simplemindedly.

"Benjy, honey, it's just time. Plus we would like some grand-kids before we leave this life," Linda explained. With that, Luther embraced her with a warm hug and a smile.

"I can take care of you and Dad," Benjamin stated.

"We are fine. In fact we were thinking about doing some traveling, spend some of our money for once," Luther added.

"But—"

"No buts. We have made our decision, and that's final," Luther interrupted.

"Mom!" he shouted, looking at his mom with childlike eyes, but Linda remained unperturbed. "Don't do this. You can't do this to me!" Benjy pleaded.

"Don't you dare raise your voice at your mother!" Luther responded sternly.

Benjamin looked at his parents with anger-filled eyes.

"We are done here, son," said Luther.

"You will regret this. I'll make you pay!" Benjamin uttered menacingly. He stormed out of his parents' office but not before violently knocking over an Egyptian vase that was perched on an ivory stand by the doorway, slammed the door shut, and was never seen again since that fateful day.

* * *

Linda and Luther decided to take that well-deserved trip they'd been talking about for years. They backpacked through Europe and had the time of their lives, just being free of all their inhibitions, exploring, and trying new things. They swam with the dolphins in Jamaica and fell in love with Bob Marley and reggae music. They ended their trip in the Great Barrier Reef in Australia, where they enjoyed the white beaches surrounded by azure seas. On the flight back home, Luther wanted to watch a movie, so he randomly picked the first one that popped up on the screen, and there he was, Benjamin Knight kicking ass in the latest action movie. Luther couldn't believe what his big beautiful hazel eyes were seeing—his eldest son whom he hadn't seen since that heartbreaking day when he stormed out of the office. Benjamin had gone on to become a famous movie star.

"Linda, Linda, look! I think it's Benjy!" Luther bellowed, frantically shaking Linda by her shoulder and then quickly apologizing to the other passengers on the airplane.

Linda covered her mouth in disbelief, and a single teardrop slowly rolled down her plump, rosy right cheek, and in that instant Luther knew what he had to do the moment they got home.

They got home on a Monday, and by Tuesday evening, Luther and Linda were sitting around the dining room table, and one by one they phoned their children. First they called Christopher.

"Christopher, its Mom and Dad," they said excitedly. For them, it was always a pleasure talking to Christopher.

"So we were thinking about having a family reunion this weekend and would love it if you could make it," Linda stated.

"Mom, you know I'll be there!" Christopher exclaimed. "Would you like me to bring anything?" he asked.

"No, just get here," said Luther.

They hung up the phone feeling pleased, feeling like they were doing the right thing, so they proceeded.

Then they called Benjamin, but the phone went unanswered, so they left a brief message. "Hi, Benjy, it's your parents. We will be having a family get-together this weekend and would love it if you could be there," said Linda.

"Love you, son," said Luther.

At the end of the call, they looked at each other doubtfully because they hadn't heard from Benjamin in years. Last but not least, they called Isabella.

"Isabella, it's Mom and Dad. How are you?" they asked simultaneously.

"Hi, Mom. Hey, Dad," Isabella replied with surprise.

"Your mom and I would love for you to come home next weekend for a family reunion. It's been too long," said Luther.

"I'll be there," Isabella replied.

"Isabella, have you spoken to Benjy lately?" Linda asked.

"Yes, I spoke to him a few days ago," she replied.

"Could you reach out to him for us? We tried calling him but got no answer," Linda said.

"I'll try, but, Mom, I can't make any promises," Isabella said, so unsure.

"Thank you," they both replied.

"Love you both, and see you then," Isabella said.

"Love you too," they replied, and with that, they ended the call.

* * *

The next day, Christopher hopped on a plane and was the first one there.

"Linda, there's a knock at the door!" shouted Luther from his office.

"I'll get it!" Linda shouted back.

She opened the door in her floral apron covered in flour. Holding the door open with her left hand, Linda leaned back, tilting her head back and over her shoulder. She screamed, "It's Christopher!"

Luther immediately got up from his desk and hurried to the door.

"Hi, Mom. Look at you," Christopher said while holding an expensive bottle of champagne in one hand and twirling his mom around with the other. "You haven't aged a day," he said.

"Oh, stop," she replied modestly.

He gave his mom a kiss on the cheek and the biggest and warmest hug. Luther came up behind Linda with an outstretched arm, which Christopher gladly took, and with a swift pull, they were interlocked in a manly hug.

"How are you, son?" Luther asked.

"Dad, you look great," said Christopher.

They all congregated in the kitchen and had some of Linda's freshly baked homemade coconut macaroon cookies.

The next day, Isabella showed up, and everyone was so excited to see one another. There were long hugs all around, and it was almost like the old times—almost. They were all so happy, but no one could deny the absence of Benjamin.

"Mom, I tried reaching out to Benjy with no luck," Isabella whispered in Linda's ear.

Linda sighed and replied, "That's OK," and gave a faint smile.

* * *

It was Saturday and also the day of the reunion party, but still no Benjamin. They all carried on as planned. The air was filled with laughter and happiness and the aroma of an array of spices and pastry. Luther was about to ask if anyone had heard from

Benjamin, but before he could, the door opened, and everyone turned around to see who it was. There stood in the doorway Benjamin Knight—six feet tall, hair slicked back, wearing a gray suit and sunglasses, and carrying a small black hand luggage.

Linda grabbed Luther's wrist, and they both looked at each other and breathed a sigh of relief. Everyone stood still in silence for a moment, including Benjamin. It was like the prodigal son had returned. The tension was unquestionably thick, but that was quickly diminished when Benjamin dropped his bag, took his shades off, and approached everyone with outstretched arms and a huge smile.

"Benjy!" Isabella shouted, pushing everyone out of her way, ran toward him, and jumped in his arms with her legs wrapped tightly around his waist. They practically had to peel her off him.

The party was in full swing now. They all sat at the dining room table, with Linda and Luther at both ends, Benjamin and Isabella on one side, and Christopher on the other side by himself, but that didn't faze Christopher because he was used to being the odd one out. The sandalwood table was buried with food, desserts, and champagne from one end to the other. They sat there for hours on end, eating, drinking, laughing, and exchanging stories of their accomplishments.

Cling! Cling! Cling! The room went hushed as everyone looked in the direction of the cling. Luther was standing at the head of the table holding up a champagne glass that was a little bit too full, with tiny air bubbles sticking to the inside of the glass.

With a proud look on his face, he said, "Now that I have all your attention, Linda and I are not getting younger as you all can tell, and so we thought it was time to make a final will and testament. We met with the lawyer and decided to split the wealth evenly among you three."

Benjamin, Isabella, and Christopher looked at one another. Luther raised his glass high and out in front of his face.

"I would like to make a toast to family, life, and happiness," he said.

Everyone raised their glasses and said harmoniously, "To family."

"Enough of that. Let's get back to the party," Linda interrupted.

After about five bottles of champagne, it was time for bed.

"Get plenty of rest, everyone. We have a big day ahead of us," Luther announced, slurring his words and out of character.

They were all walking into walls and chairs, but they managed to drag themselves to bed.

The next day, they were all hungover. After breakfast they packed up the truck for their family hike, but at the last minute, Benjamin withdrew.

"I'm not feeling too good," he claimed.

"It's not like we are feeling ourselves either," said Christopher.

"I know, but I feel like I'm going to puke any minute now."

"The fresh air will do you some good," Linda added.

Huuuuurggehh! Benjamin covered his mouth and turned his head away off to the side. In a muffled tone, he said, "I really think I should stay home, and I could make lunch until you guys get back."

"Since you insist," Linda said, disappointed.

"It better be something good," Isabella said assertively.

"Don't worry. That's the first thing I learned to do when I left home," Benjamin made it known. That ugly fight he had with his parents the day he left home flashed in his memory, and anger flashed in his eyes. When he quickly realized what was happening to him, he shook his head, blinked his eyes, and came back to reality. He gave a fake smile to his family, who was looking at him with concern all over their faces.

"Go, go. I got this," Benjamin reassured them.

They got the rest of their stuff and headed on their journey. Benjamin watched on and waved as they drove off into the thick early morning fog. Benjamin disappeared into the house as Isabella looked back one last time from the back seat of the truck.

The Knight family got to the end of their three-mile hike, at the top of a mountain that overlooked a ravine. They all took a few minutes to admire the different chirping sounds of the birds and the beauty of the trees as the rising sun peeked in through their branches and leaves. Christopher stepped closer to the edge to get a better look. He closed his eyes and tilted his head back as a ray of sunlight hit him perfectly in the face. Isabella glared at him menacingly. She walked up behind him, startling him and causing his right leg to slip out from underneath him. She grabbed him by the arm and pulled him back before he went over.

"You should be more careful," she whispered.

With his heart pounding out of his chest and fright written all over his face, Christopher replied, "Right."

He looked around at his parents, but Luther was showing Linda a red-and-black woodpecker high up on a tree, pecking away at the wood, so they hadn't noticed what was unfolding behind them.

"Guys, I think we should head back," Christopher called out.

"Right, lunch should be ready by now," said Linda.

"I wonder what Benjy's making," Isabella chimed in.

They started making the hour-long drive home. Twenty minutes into the drive, a few drops of rain sprinkled on the windshield, and then out of nowhere, it started to rain cats and dogs. Luther was the one behind the wheel. It was raining so hard. There were little to no visibility. The truck started to swerve violently from one side of the road to the other. Screams echoed from the back seat of the car where Linda and Isabella sat. They all thought it was a good idea for Christopher to sit up front with Luther so they could get some more father-and-son time. They were fortunate because there wasn't any oncoming traffic at that terrifying moment. Luther made the critical decision to pull off to the side of the road until it stopped raining. They played car charades while they waited for the rain to die down.

"Look, it stopped raining," Linda pointed out.

"Let's go home," said Luther.

So Luther slowly and carefully got the truck back on the road. Linda's favorite song, "Running Man Bible," exhilarated them as they all sang along. The truck went down a hill, around a sharp corner; upon clearing the corner, the truck lost all break functionality. Everything happened so fast Luther didn't even have time to react until it was too late. He tried to keep the truck on the road by steering it out of the embankment, but he turned the steering wheel too hard and too fast, causing the truck to slam head-on into a tree on the opposite side of the road.

Christopher was knocked unconscious by the impact. When he came to, he was disoriented, his vision was blurry, his head was throbbing, and there was something running down his face. Christopher slowly wiped his fingers across his forehead and then held it up in front of his half-opened eyes, and that was when he realized that blood was gushing out from his head. He tried moving, but there was a sharp, stabbing pain in his back, causing him to let out gut-wrenching screams. Suddenly, he heard moaning and groaning coming from the left of him. He managed to pick his head up, and that was when he saw what was left of his parents' truck.

The truck was wrapped around a huge English oak tree, white smoke coming up from its engine. All the windows were shattered, and there was blood dripping from a few pieces of windshield glass that was still left intact. Luther was slumped over the steering wheel; his glasses were crumpled up on his face, and his right arm was twisted up in an unnatural way behind his back. Linda was in the passenger seat behind Luther. A black gaping hole remained where her left eye used to be, and her head was resting on Isabella's shoulder while the rest of her body was held straight upright by a tree branch, which impaled her in the middle of her chest. Her clothes were saturated in her own blood. Both Isabella's legs were fractured in several places. Her neck got snapped by her seat belt upon the truck's impact with the tree. There was a long black burn mark behind her ear that went down the right side of her neck and under her chin, where the seat belt had burned into her flesh.

* * *

A woman in her mid-thirties, about the same age as Christopher, and her white Siberian husky were driving down the road when they came to a screeching halt. She jumped out of her Jeep Wrangler to discover Christopher lying on the side of the road, clinging to life. She immediately called for help, all while trying to keep Christopher awake.

"Sir, hold on, stay with me," she said.

"My...fam—" Christopher said, trying to speak, but he was too weak.

"Sir, don't speak. I'll check on your family," she replied.

Her angelic voice caressed Christopher's ears and gave him enough energy to fight for his life. The woman went over to check on the remaining passengers, and what she saw was horrifying. She hurried back over to Christopher's side, thinking all the other passengers were already dead; she held his hand until rescue arrived.

"Sir, hold on. I can hear sirens," she encouraged him.

The ambulance finally arrived, and they immediately rushed Christopher and his family to the hospital.

Benjamin was at home making his famous island duck with mulberry mustard when he got a phone call, urging him to come to the hospital right away—his family was in an accident, and they might not make it. A devastated Benjamin dropped the wooden spoon he was using to stir the sauce, turned off the stove, and bolted to his car. He swung the car door open, hopped in, slammed the door shut, put his seat belt on, and went to switch the car on when he realized he didn't have his keys. He ran back to the house, retrieved his keys, and hauled his ass over to the hospital, which was only twenty minutes away. He got to the help desk ten minutes later and presented his identification, and then they immediately escorted him into a private room. The doctor took a deep breath then entered the room and closed the door behind him. He clasped his hands, interlocking his fingers tightly. He sat Benjamin down and delivered unto him a grim revelation.

"Mr. Knight, I am deeply sorry to be bringing you this heart-breaking news. Your mom, sister, and dad have all passed away due to the injuries they have sustained. Your brother is still in surgery and in critical condition. They are doing everything they can to save him," said the doctor with trembling voice.

Benjamin put his face in his hands on his lap and just sat there in silence.

The doctor walked over to him and put his hand on Benjamin's shoulder and said, "If there's anything at all that I can get you, please don't hesitate to let me know."

Benjamin just sat there in disbelief.

* * *

It took three months and fifteen days for Christopher to regain his mobility and reenter into society. You would think that Benjamin would have been happy to see his brother out of the hospital, but he was more interested in the inheritance he stood to gain from the unexpected passing of almost his entire family. Benjamin called a meeting with Christopher and the family's lawyer to divulge their parents' last will and testament. The lawyer, wearing a sharp gray suit, entered the family office.

"I am terribly sorry for your loss," he said, placing a golden case on the table, which he then unlocked with a very unique-looking key. He pulled out several pieces of papers and a recorder.

"For the record, in the presence of Christopher Knight and Benjamin Knight, I will read the last will and testament of Luther and Linda Knight," he said before he began. "To our beloved Isabella, we leave all of Linda's jewelry, which is worth over one billion dollars, and in the event that anything happens to Isabella, the jewelry should be set aside for our grandchildren. To our dear Benjamin, we leave the mansion he loved so much and the horses. And to our youngest, Christopher, we leave our multibillion-dollar companies for him to do as he sees fit," the lawyer concluded.

There was an awkward pause.

"Where's the rest of it?" Benjamin asked.

"That's all of it," the lawyer replied.

Benjamin picked up the golden case and flipped it upside down, but nothing else was inside. He slammed it back down on the table. "At the party, Dad said they were sharing everything evenly," Benjamin said uncomprehendingly.

"I hear what you are saying, and I understand your frustration. Your parents did call me to speak briefly about the changes they wish to make, but that tragic accident happened before they could get to my office and make those changes official, so my hands are tied, and I have to go along with the original will and testament," the lawyer explained.

"So all that was for nothing," Benjamin murmured, folding his arms and flopping back in his chair, very childlike.

Christopher and the lawyer both looked at each other, not sure of what they just heard.

"What was that?" Christopher asked, but Benjamin had nothing more to say.

The lawyer turned over the deeds and bid the men farewell. Benjamin stormed out of the office, and Christopher went back to life as he knew it before all this tragedy and misfortune.

* * *

Five years after Luther, Linda, and Isabella passed away, Benjamin still could not get over his parents' final will and testament, so he literally drank himself to death. Christopher got a surprising phone call, instructing him to come to the family's mansion to claim the mansion and its contents. When he got there, he was informed that Benjamin had overdosed on drugs and alcohol. At that point, Christopher decided to move back into the family's mansion.

One day Christopher was at the grocery store, over in the produce section. He was looking down at his shopping list while reaching to his left for a mango when he accidentally grabbed a hand. He quickly took his eyes off the list and apologized for being absentminded. The person whose hand he grabbed assured him that she would not hold it against him. The moment the first word rolled out of her lips, it was like music to his ears, and he thought, *I know that voice*, but he couldn't remember from where.

"Do I know you?" he asked.

"I don't think so," she replied, squinting as she tried to think.

"Well, I'm Christopher Knight," he said, reaching for a handshake.

"Hi, Christopher Knight. I'm Jade Lloyd," she said as she shook his hand.

Christopher instantly felt electricity running through his body, and she felt it too because they both pulled their hands back and looked at each other as if to check if the other felt it too.

As a little girl growing up, Jade Lloyd was vibrant and full of life. She had the kindest voice you had ever heard. Her childhood wasn't always rainbows and butterflies. Poverty was evident and also the color of her skin. Her family didn't have a lot, but you wouldn't know that by just looking at her because she always wore the brightest smile.

* * *

Christopher and Jade saw each other again and again at that same grocery store. Each time they exchanged hellos and went on their ways. One day Christopher made the life-changing decision to ask her out because he just couldn't shake the feeling that he knew her from somewhere, not to mention that undeniable spark they both felt when they touched.

"We have to stop meeting like this," Christopher called out to Jade.

"Oh hi, Christopher. Didn't see you there," she replied.

"I think you should grab a drink with me," he said with a smile.

"Is that right? If I didn't know any better, I would say you are flirting with me, Mr. Knight."

"So is that a yes, Ms. Lloyd?" he asked.

"One drink," she replied.

That one drink turned into a routine, which led to a relationship that had both of them feeling like they were teenagers again. They were inseparable; they often took long walks hand in hand. Christopher would touch Jade every chance he got. He couldn't keep his hands off her. The love they slowly cultivated bloomed into a sweet bed of beautiful roses, which they shared for several years. One day they were sharing stories of their past, and it was at that moment that Christopher knew where he had heard Jade's voice before. Jade was the woman with the angelic voice who stopped to help him when he was in that devastating car accident that claimed the lives of half his family. Jade was right there then, and she was right there now.

* * *

Misfortune stuck again, but this time Jade was at the losing end. Christopher was diagnosed with a rare form of brain cancer, which he developed after the car accident. And he was deteriorating fast. Before they knew it, he was bedbound, with Jade right by his side, caring for him. The cancer was ravaging his body faster than they had time to spend together, and even though Christopher didn't look like his old handsome self, Jade never let him forget how much she loved him and would do anything for him. Christopher wasn't afraid to let it be known that no other woman had ever made him feel the way Jade did—the way she made the hair on the back of his neck stand in excitement, the way his toes curled in pleasurable moments, and that tingle of electricity that ran throughout his entire body whenever her delicate warm lips met his. Christopher never failed to remind her, and Jade wasn't shy about not letting him forget it either.

Jade sat on the bed facing him. She placed his hand over her heart and her hand over his heart. She leaned over and gently whispered in his ear, "You will always be my one and only love." And she sealed it with a kiss.

"You will always be my last love," he mustered all his strength and whispered back.

They both laughed because even in death he still had a sense of humor.

* * *

A few short weeks later, Christopher was taking his last breath in his mansion bedroom with Jade right by his side, but not before sharing a secret that he had been holding on to all these years. "I have a daughter, but she's away getting treatment. I'm sorry. I love you."

With his conscience clear, his soul slipped away from his body. His eyes were still open, so Jade slowly closed them as she kissed him on the forehead. "Rest well, my love," she whispered.

Even though Jade and Christopher shared a union, she would not be sharing in his wealth. The daughter Christopher mentioned on his deathbed would stand to inherit it all as his last will and testament stated. And that treatment he mentioned was in fact rehab—the girl was an addict. Christopher was ashamed of what she became, so he wouldn't talk about her. It was a good thing Jade Lloyd wasn't in it for the money. Jade, being the kindhearted person that she was, moved out of the mansion and moved on with her life without a fuss. Meanwhile, daddy's unstable little girl came home to claim all his riches.

Love doesn't always conquer all.

THE END

The Con Artist

"I don't want to see you back here, Mr. Savage, because next time you won't get off this easily," the judge warned.

Joe Savage left the court room feeling like he just won again. He wasn't always on the wrong side of the law. In high school, Joe Savage was a straight A student. He also attended one of the most decorated colleges in the United States, Yale University. One night Joe got into a horrid bar fight when the cops were called to the scene. Somehow Joe Savage charmed his way out of any and all charges with his baby blue eyes, pearly white teeth, and perfect smile. After that, Joe found his calling, or so he thought.

Joe was all smiles leaving the courthouse. He was so happy that he had a bounce in his step, his chest erected and striding as though he was on top of the world. Walking backward, looking up at the courthouse with his jacket swung over his shoulder, not paying attention to where he was going, he bumped into a blond bombshell, sending papers flying. With her perfect figure, she stood at five feet six inches. She was wearing a short fitted black skirt suit, red pumps, and bright red lipstick. They both quickly retrieved the papers before they were carried away by the wind. As Joe was handing her a piece of the papers, he paused and looked deeply into her alluring green eyes.

"Maybe you should watch where you are going," Joe said.

"Maybe you shouldn't walk backward," she snapped back.

To Joe, it was as if time was going in slow motion as he stared at her lips as she spoke. He didn't hear a word she said, and she didn't know what else to say. They burst out laughing. She gathered the rest of her papers, and then they parted ways. Destiny Burns, who was about to graduate law school, was heading to the courthouse for her first day of internship.

* * *

Weeks later, Destiny was at her favorite hangout spot. She often went to Russo's bar, just to unwind after a long day at work.

"The usual?" the bartender asked.

"No, surprise me," she replied.

The bartender, with his gelled hair, chiseled jawbone, and perfect tanned skin, was wearing a T-shirt that looked to be two sizes too small that you could see every single ab muscle perfectly protruding through his shirt. He made her a whiskey sour, and she was pleased. Destiny tended to attract a lot of unwanted attention, and tonight was one of those nights.

As she sipped on her new favorite drink, all sorts of men were coming at her left and right, and she would turn them down as they approached before they could even take a seat. She was starting to get annoyed, so she swiveled on her barstool, turning her back to the crowd; she held a finger up, gesturing to the bartender for one more drink. She looked to her left, and there was a tall, dark, handsome drink of chocolate milk sitting next to her. He stretched his hand out to introduce himself.

"Hi. I'm Nate," he said.

As she was about to reply, someone came up behind her, placed both hands on her shoulder, and whispered in her ear, "Hey, honey," then gave her a kiss on the cheek. It was none other than Joe Savage swooping in to rescue her. He was watching her all night from across the room. Nate shook his head then got up and left, and Joe took his seat.

They chatted, laughed, and drank all night. Before they knew it, it was 1:00 a.m., and they were both stumbling out of the bar holding each other up, laughing uncontrollably, and slurring their words. They got to her apartment door, and Destiny fumbled for her keys as Joe kissed the back of her neck. They managed to make it to the bed, kissing, bumping into walls, and knocking over a vase on their way there. They got to the bed, and they both fell in, Joe on top of Destiny. Joe took his time slowly removing her clothes, and with each article of clothing he removed, he kissed her body in places that made her felt like she was floating on cloud nine. Destiny never dreamed that someone could make her feel so much pleasure in just one night. That night, Destiny had the best sex she ever had in years, and Joe was doing what Joe did best, literally charming the pants off the ladies.

The following day, Destiny was awoken by sunlight beaming in her eyes through the window curtains of her studio apartment. She rolled over onto her side with a huge smile on her face, reaching out to touch Joe on the other side of the bed, but it was cold and empty. Joe was gone, and so were all her bank cards. She was left with a killer hangover, a very expensive bar bill, and a void bank account. The proof was in the receipt on the nightstand next to the bed. Destiny grabbed the receipt and stared at it wide eyed in disbelief. Great sex suddenly turned into great regret.

Destiny tried tirelessly to forget about Joe Savage and the disgust she felt every time she thought about that night. It was months before they finally ran into each other again, and they both acted as though nothing had happened between them. They said hello and quickly said their goodbyes then went on their ways. Seeing Joe made Destiny relive that night all over again. So much pleasure but yet so much pain. Destiny wasn't always treated fairly, she wasn't well liked, and she was always picked on and bullied, especially in high school. Every time she thought about Joe and that night, it made her sick to her stomach because it brought her back to her high school days. She thought how satisfying it would be to make him pay for what he did to her, but she could never muster up enough courage to even tell him how she really felt.

Destiny hadn't seen Joe at the courthouse anymore, so that meant he must be staying out of trouble for once in his adult life. And that was true; after that night, Joe Savage attempted to turn his life around. It was like he had a wake-up call and decided to clean up his act. One day Joe was having lunch with an old college buddy of his when he got a phone call. The voice on the other end of the line was so unrecognizable it almost sounded like a poor network connection. He couldn't tell if the voice belonged to a male or a female, but what was clear was what the voice said next.

"You have one simple task to complete, and if you refuse to do so, I will expose you to the world and to that college buddy of yours for what you really are," said the voice.

Joe was a man who cared about his image and what people thought of him. After hearing all that, Joe knew he was being watched, so he became paranoid and started looking around at everyone suspiciously. It seemed as though everyone was on their cell phones at that very moment, so it was hard to tell if the voice came from someone nearby.

"One second," Joe said to his buddy and got up from the table. "Who is this?" he asked.

"Who is not important. It's the what," the voice replied.

"What is it you want from me?" asked Joe.

"I need you to break into the art museum, retrieve the original painting of the *Mona Lisa*, and replace it with the fake painting; I will provide to you at a later date, should you choose to accept. So what will it be, Mr. Savage?" the voice asked.

Knowing all the unspeakable things that Joe had done, he had no choice but to go forward with what the voice wanted him to do. "Fine, fine, I'll do it," Joe said without hesitation.

"I'll be in touch, and don't even think about leaving town or calling the cops."

Then there was silence. With his back still turned to his buddy, Joe put his phone in his pocket, regained his composure, and returned to the table with a fake smile on his face as if everything was OK.

* * *

It was weeks later before Joe heard anything from the voice. He got a text message instructing him where to pick up the replacement *Mona Lisa*. He read the message, and after ten seconds, the message was automatically deleted. Now it was time for Joe to start making plans on how to make the impossible possible. So he spent night after night watching the museum and the guards' every move. There was this one guard in particular who worked four nights every week, so he was there the most, and he also looked like an easy target for Joe.

One night, while Joe was staking out the museum, he saw this particular guard coming in for work, so he hurried over to him and struck up a conversation. "Excuse me, sir," Joe called out.

"Hi, how may I help you?" the guard asked.

"I was wondering if you could help me figure out how to read this map. I'm not from the area," he replied.

"Yeah, sure. Where are you trying to go?" the guard asked.

"A friend of mine is having an art show in the area that I was trying to get to," said Joe.

"Art show? Where at?" asked the guard.

"She said it was at a location not too far from here, um..." Joe tried to come up with a name.

"Oh, it must be at the Winford Theater," the guard suggested, not realizing that Joe was a trickster.

"Yes, that's the one," Joe confirmed.

"OK, take the first two rights, then at the stoplight make a left, and the building should be on your left, in front of the old Baptist church," the guard directed.

"Thank you, sir. You've been very helpful," Joe said sincerely.

While the guard was doing his best to get Joe to where he was supposedly going, Joe was carefully slipping off the guard's keys from the key chain that hung from his back pocket. Using his slender fingers, Joe made copies then returned them without the naive guard knowing.

* * *

One Sunday Joe bumped into the guard at the grocery store and struck up yet another conversation. He invited Joe over for Sunday dinner with him and his wife, and Joe gladly accepted. They had ham, mashed potatoes, and a side of green beans with about two and a half bottles of red wine. Man, that guard went to town; he told Joe everything he needed to know about the museum, and Joe absorbed it like a sponge.

"The museum is heavily guarded with two security guards posted at the entrance every night, security cameras at every turn, and laser beam cages that activate whenever someone or something gets too close to the artifacts," the guard pointed out.

Joe would have to play his cards right, or else he would get caught in the act. Now Joe had everything he needed to retrieve the painting, so the voice instructed him to go ahead and break into the museum.

* * *

On Saturday, August 23, the air was so thick you could practically taste it. It was a slow night at the museum, and Joe was lurking outside waiting for his opportunity to get in unnoticed. He was covered in an all-black outfit from head to toe, with the fake painting strapped to his back. His outfit was almost like a second skin. A delivery truck was approaching the gate, which gave Joe the perfect opportunity to get in. The truck stopped at the gate. The driver showed his ID to the guard, who looked at it very carefully with his flashlight, and everything seemed to check out, so he returned it to the driver. Joe carefully slipped under the truck and attached himself to the bottom of it. The driver was then instructed to pull the truck around to the loading dock, which was at the east end of the museum. When the truck came to a stop, Joe made his way out from underneath it, and as soon as the doors opened, he slid inside like a snake without being noticed.

Once inside, Joe located a map of the museum right where the guard said it would be. He remembered overhearing one of the guards telling the other that he was having to reboot the security system, and it would take about five minutes to get it back up and running, so he quickly made his way to the *Mona Lisa*. Joe carefully swapped out the paintings and was about to make his getaway when he saw flashing lights and heard voices. It was the guards making rounds while the system was down. Joe stood there frozen with nowhere to go. With panic and desperation setting in, Joe started to sweat profusely under his ninja suit. He threw his head back as if to give up, and that was when he saw an air vent up above him. Being the resourceful person he was, Joe made his way up into the vent and closed it right as the guards rounded the corner. The guards stopped beneath the vent and shone their flashlights on the *Mona Lisa*. They paused for a second, and then they both looked at each other.

"Does her eyes look off to you?" asked one guard.

The other guard shrugged and replied, "They look fine to me."

As the guards turned to walk away, a single drop of Joe's sweat rolled down his nose and off his face and landed just on the tip of the guard's navy blue baseball cap. When the guards were out of sight, Joe climbed down and escaped through the same way he came in, with the original *Mona Lisa* tethered to his back.

Once out of sight of the museum, Joe breathed a sigh of relief. Suddenly, his phone rang, and it was none other than the voice on the other end.

"You have my painting?" questioned the voice.

"Yes," Joe replied reluctantly.

"OK, go home and wait for further instructions," commanded the voice.

Without another word, the call was disconnected. Once home, Joe sat on his couch and nervously flipped through the local news stations to see if there was any mention of the missing painting. As he couldn't sit still, Joe paced back and forth in his living room, asking himself, "What have I just done?" Joe was on edge, literally on the edge of his chair, phone in hand, waiting for his next move when he saw flashing blue lights out of his peripheral vision. He jumped onto his feet, pacing even faster with both hands on his head and swearing like a sailor. He was punching a hole in his living room wall when he heard the loudest three knocks he had ever heard in his life. He took a big gulp and opened the door. The life drained from his face; he was as pale as a ghost.

The officers shone their flashlights directly in Joe's face; he squinted and covered his face with the back of his hand ever so slightly.

"Good evening, sir. Sorry to bother you this late, but we got an anonymous tip about the missing *Mona Lisa*, and we need to take a look around," the officer stated.

Joe's heart sank to the bottom of his feet because he knew that the painting was right there on his dining room table. With nowhere to run, Joe had no choice but to comply with the officer's request. He backed away from the door, and they entered. They looked around with their tiny flashlights, and lo and behold, there was the *Mona Lisa*, nicely laid out on the table for them to find. Joe took one more deep breath and stretched both hands out in front of him, waiting to be handcuffed. They read him his rights while putting him in the back of the patrol car. Joe hung his head in regret as he was being hauled off to jail.

The very next day, he was brought before the very same judge who warned him not to come back in her courtroom. It was Joe Savage versus the state of New York. Representing the state was none other than Destiny Burns. Cold sweat washed over Joe, and he almost passed out when he saw her looking as stunning as she was the day they first met. She entered the courtroom with such confidence, as if she was strutting the runway at the New York Fashion Week wearing a navy blue pantsuit. With a cold stare, she looked dead straight into Joe's captivating blue eyes, and without a word or smile, she took her place on the right side of the courtroom.

"All rise. The honorable judge Grace presides! You may be seated," said the bailiff.

"Mr. Savage, didn't I warn you not to come back here?" Judge Grace said sternly.

"Your Honor, there's no proof that my client was ever in that museum," Joe's lawyer stated.

"Your Honor, if I may?" Destiny asked.

"Go ahead, Ms. Burns," the judge ordered.

"Your Honor, I present exhibit A." Destiny pulled out a blue baseball cap—the guard's to be exact, the very same one the guard at the museum was wearing that night. "Your Honor, on this hat is a single drop of the defendant's DNA." Destiny brought the hat to the judge's bench, along with the results of a DNA analysis, which declared that the DNA found on the tip of the baseball cap was in fact Joe's.

Joe slowly hung his head as he realized that he would not be charming his way out of this predicament he found himself in. The judge reviewed the evidence and ruled that there was no need for any further testimony or deliberation.

"Mr. Savage is to serve ten years in federal lockup."

She slammed the gavel down, and Joe shifted in his chair. He knew there was no coming back this time.

"Court is dismissed," said the judge, and then she exited the courtroom.

On her way out of the courtroom, Destiny leaned over and whispered in Joe's ear, "You will always be a savage, but I'm destiny." She then walked away and never looked back.

Joe's eyes enlarged, for right then and there, he realized that the voice on the phone and Destiny were the same person.

While in lockup, Joe Savage was already planning his escape. Even though he tried to turn his life around, deep down, Joe will always be a *savage*.

Don't mess with destiny. You might just get burned.

THE END

The Confession...Letter

There was nothing but a sliver of light seeping through the cracks of the door.

"Shhh!" she said.

"We are going to get caught," he whispered.

"We are only going to get caught if you don't shut up and kiss me," she replied in a boss-like tone.

As her warm, voluptuous, soft lips met his slightly wet lips, both their eyes slowly closed, and they melted into each other. At that very moment, it was as if it was just the two of them that existed. There was no chatter on the other side of that door, no noise whatsoever, and it was completely and utterly silent. With both her hands pressing firmly up against his back, his right hand gently caressed the side of her neck as his left fingertips slowly crept down her body and came to a rest just on the small of her back. They shared a passionate kiss that neither one of them could get enough of. There were a lot of moments with weak knees and hearts bursting with excitement. After a few electrifying minutes, which felt like hours, they both exited the secret doorway of the clubhouse one at a time, straightening their clothes as they reunited with some of the most elite people you could name.

No woman, or anyone for that matter, had ever taken charge of him like that. He had always been his own boss his whole life. Alex Solo, and his name said it all, was a self-made businessman who had never depended on anyone's help to be as successful as he was. He owned several businesses all over the country and a few in foreign countries such as Switzerland and Spain. When he entered a room, most of the time, he was the most aristocratic man, and he knew it, but he never let that get to his head. He remained humble and down to earth.

Alex Solo surrounded himself with like-minded people and with the finest things in life. So he was surprised when he became drawn to Naima Jay Marie the instant he laid eyes on her curvaceous figure, I mean her beautiful face when she walked into one of his coffee shops that morning in her rose pink pajamas. She wasn't frowned upon for wearing her pajamas because the name of the coffee shop was The Lounge, and that was exactly what you do. You wear your pajamas and you lounge while having great coffee. Her face was beautifully flawless without even a drop of makeup on. Her smooth caramel skin fit seamlessly in her two-piece pajamas, her curly honey blond hair tucked away on top of her head in a messy bun. She had the perfect lips, if he ever did see one.

She was for sure admiring him as well. He caught her looking in his direction several times. They didn't recognize each other because the first time they met was at a masquerade party, where they had a brief but steamy interaction in a very dark room, when they were both young and single. Their eyes locked, and they both gave each other a smile from across the room. She quickly turned her head away to hide the fact that she was blushing, and Alex was left wondering what was coming over him. At that moment, he didn't have an answer for himself, but he wasn't going to waste time trying to figure it out either because she was finished with her coffee and was about to head out the door.

It was now or never. He grabbed a breakfast pastry and made a mad dash toward the door.

"Excuse me!" he called out.

She turned to see what the fuss was about.

"You forgot to take your complimentary breakfast pastry," Alex said while handing her a glazed croissant.

"Oh, thank you," she said with a smile and turned to walk away.

Alex grabbed her pinkie finger tenderly and said, "Wait, I couldn't help but notice that you were here by yourself."

"Yes, I am," she replied.

"And why is that? No significant other?" he asked.

"I like to have breakfast alone sometimes," she explained.

"Would you like to have your pastry with me while I have my coffee? I don't like to have breakfast alone," he said with flirtation written all over his face.

"No significant other, Mr....?"

"It's Solo, Alex Solo. And you are?"

"It's Jay Marie, Naima Jay Marie," she replied sarcastically.

"Shall we?" Alex asked, gesturing to a table by the window.

"We shall," she said blushingly.

They sat by the window and indulged in sticky breakfast pastry and creamy delicious coffee. But that wasn't the only thing Alex was enjoying; he was gazing deeply into Naima's eyes as the morning sun shone upon her. Their conversation was so effortless, like two people who have known and understood each other for years. They understood each other's sarcasm and playfulness. They made each other laugh without even trying. Their conversation went on without them realizing how much time had passed.

"Oh shoot!" she yelled.

"What is it?" Alex yelled back.

"I'm going to be late for that thing," she said, searching for her words.

"That thing, really?" he said.

"Yes, really," she replied.

"OK, at least let me walk you to your car," Alex offered.

"Yeah, sure," she quickly accepted.

So they got up and walked to the door.

Alex opened the door and said, "Here you go, my lady."

"Thank you, sir," she replied.

They walked to her red BMW, and of course Alex opened the door for her. She got in and rolled the window down.

"Hey, would you like to go to that thing with me? I'm sorry, don't answer that. I'm sure you are a very busy man and you have better things to do." She quickly changed her mind.

"No take backs," he said very excitedly, and before she could say another word, he was already in the front seat with his seat belt on.

"So where to, my lady?" he asked.

"You'll see," she replied mysteriously.

For the entire fifteen-minute drive, Alex couldn't take his eyes off her. They pulled into a parking lot.

"We're here," she said.

"Here, where is here?" Alex asked.

"In that building over there." She pointed to a brightly painted building. "I visit kids with special needs."

Alex looked at her very impressed and very lustfully. Then he said, "This might sound strange and out of nowhere, but I would..." He paused.

"Would what?" she asked.

"I really would love to kiss you right now," he confessed.

"Well..." She paused.

He then removed his seat belt, reached over, and caressed the side of her face, and they both leaned in for the kiss that would change everything. They are face-to-face, nose-to-nose, breath-to-breath, and then it happened. She surrendered fully to having all her senses entwined with the hunk on the other end of her lips. After their lips finally separated, with twinkle in her brown eyes, Naima looked at Alex as though he was everything she had ever hoped for in a man. An intoxicated feeling washed over her entire body; if she were standing, she probably would have fallen to the ground because she was so weak in the knees. Her eyes were glossed over, and her pulse was slightly elevated. She hadn't felt this kind of excitement in a very long time, but it would come at a price.

"I can stop if you would like me to," Alex suggested.

"I shouldn't do this. I think we should..."

But before she could finish that sentence, their lips were interlocked again, with sparks flying, hearts racing, and palms sweating. The guilt was so thick in her gut; it was almost like a bolt of lightning hitting her in the stomach, and she pushed him off and told him that she really shouldn't be doing this. Then she drove him back to the coffee shop where they met.

When they got to the coffee shop, Alex opened the door, but he hesitated to get out.

"Could I at least have your number?" he asked.

"Nope, but you could give me yours," she replied, so he did.

"What, now I'm just supposed to wait for you to contact me?" he asked.

She just raised her brows and smiled. He got out of the car and shut the door, and she drove away while looking back in the rearview mirror.

The next day, Alex patiently awaited hearing from her; he checked his phone every single hour to no avail. A few more days passed and he still hadn't heard from her. She picked up her phone several times to text him, but she couldn't make herself do it, even though he was all that she could think about. After approximately five days of delaying the inevitable, she couldn't resist any longer. She reached for her phone on her work desk, and very slowly she typed, "So I was wondering if the owner of this phone would be available for coffee, around five-ish? If not, that's OK." She then hit Send.

It wasn't even twenty seconds later and her phone was already buzzing, and of course it was Alex replying.

"I have something in mind that is better than coffee. How does seven-ish sound?"

She very reluctantly agreed, and then she sent a second text—not to Alex but to her husband. "I will be a little late today, so you can eat dinner without me. I am just going to grab something at the office."

Seven o'clock in the evening rolled around, and Alex was outside waiting for Naima. He was dressed to impress in a white long-sleeved button-down shirt. Two buttons at the very top were left undone, giving a little peekaboo action. His shirt was tucked into black fitted dress pants that cut off just above the ankles, and the look was completed with a pair of pointy, shiny black dress shoes. Alex was leaning up against his white convertible, with both hands barely fitting in his pants pocket; his legs were crossed at the ankles. His head was down, and as she approached him, his head slowly rose like a dramatic scene out of a romance movie.

Alex took both Naima's hands in his, gave her a kiss on the cheek, and complimented her on her looks. "You look great out of your pajamas." He then ushered her into the front seat of his car. They drove and talked for a little over thirty minutes, then they pulled into a parking lot, which was empty, and she thought that was strange, but she didn't say anything about it. The building they pulled up to was an old graffiti brick building with a single steel door off to the side. Alex walked behind Naima with his hands covering her eyes. From the outside, it didn't look like much, but once inside, she was taken aback after he removed his hands from her eyes to unveil the private dinner and art show he had set up for just the two of them. Tears threatened to fall from her eyes as she pushed the guilt down that was nudging at her heartstring, but even then, that wasn't enough to make her call it quits right then and there. She went along with it, and as the evening progressed, she became more and more captivated by Alex and him by her.

The night was coming to an end, but Alex had one more surprise in store. On their way home, he stopped on a cliff that overlooked the entire city. They got out and stood near the edge, admiring the lights. It was like looking off into the galaxy and the endless possibilities that could come from this friendship, love affair, whatever it was that was going on between them. He stood behind her, gently rubbing her shoulders, and suddenly, the rubbing got more and more intense. He slowly slid one hand down the front of her neck and down her chest. As his hand made its way down her chest, his pinky finger pushed her blouse away as it separated her cleavage. She grabbed his hand, but he didn't stop there. He swung her around with such intensity, and their bodies slammed up against each other. Filled with sexual intent, he pressed his warm, slightly open lips against her moisturized lips, and then they plunged into the most passionate kiss ever. As temperatures rose, the fear of getting caught lowered. He kissed and softly bit her lower lip. She let her head gently fall backward, moaning softly as a trail of slow kisses went down her neck. She pushed him up against his car, and the fireworks continued. His hand gradually inched its way between her legs and up her tight pink dress while he simultaneously kissed her. The warm sensation of her skin got warmer the higher up his hand got, and as he was about to touch her in forbidden places, the ring of her phone startled them both. She swallowed hard, took a few seconds to straighten her clothes, and composed herself before she answered it.

"Hey, honey, are you OK? It's getting late. Where are you?" her husband asked.

"Yeah, I'm OK. Leaving the office right now," she replied with an unsteady voice.

"You sound different. Are you sure you're OK?" he asked again.

"I'm fine. I'll be home shortly," she tried to assure him.

After she hung up, she and Alex both looked at each other in horror, for now she would have to come clean about the other side of her life she tried to keep a secret.

"I have to go home now," she said.

"Who was that? Is everything OK?" Alex asked.

"Everything's fine, but we need to go."

They immediately got in the car, and he drove her back to her office so she could get her car. They said their goodbyes, and she opened the car door. Naima had one foot out the car when Alex grabbed her arm, and they both stared into each other's eyes before lunging at each other. Their lips met in the middle, and it was like a volcano of emotions had erupted, but it was cut short when she pulled away and said, "I really have to go."

He gave her one last kiss on the forehead, and then they parted ways.

When she got home, she headed straight for the shower, trying to wash away the guilty pleasures of her and Alex's evening while her husband awaited in their bedroom. In the shower, the warm water rolled down her body, which triggered a flashback of when Alex's hand crept slowly up her thighs, and her eyes then rolled back at the thought of it all. Meanwhile, Alex was at home in bed, lying on his back, looking up at the ceiling in amazement and disbelief about how much he was falling for her.

The next day at work, Naima could hardly contain herself; she was suddenly feeling like a woman who was finding love for the first time. She would get butterflies every time Alex's name crossed her mind. She felt like she was in a dream state, but even though the feeling for him was so intense, she spent the next few days trying to deny herself of him. He would call and text her every day, but she wouldn't give into the temptation. This game of cat and mouse went on for a week until she couldn't take it anymore, so she called him, but it wasn't the call that he was hoping for.

"I have a confession to make. I haven't been completely honest with you. I can't do this anymore, whatever this is. I'm married, and my husband is a good man who doesn't deserve any of it. Now that being said, I think that this should be the end of any and all contact between us. I can't see you or talk to you anymore," she said with regret so strong in her voice.

"I have a confession too. That day when I first saw you, I didn't expect to fall for you so quickly, but that's not all—"

She cut him off before he could say any more.

Alex was struggling with not being able to come clean to her, so a week later, he showed up at her office, waiting outside for her to get off work. She walked outside not expecting to find him looking so handsome as can be, waiting for her.

"What are you doing here? I have nothing more to say to you," she said and turned to walk to her car.

He took a few big strides and caught up with her. "Wait, wait, just give me a second," he begged.

"OK. You have one minute," she reluctantly agreed.

"I have something to show you, and I promise I will explain everything to you," he said.

"I already told you, I have a husband, and once we cross that line, there's no coming back from it. We have already blurred the lines, so let's not cross them," she warned. When Naima looked at Alex, she didn't see the blurred line; she just saw his perfect smile, his well-kept body, his impeccable fashion sense, and not to mention his smell of warm brown sugar and vanilla. All she wanted was for him to embrace her, but she resisted the urge.

When he looked at her, he saw a gorgeous woman whom he could possibly spend the rest of his life with, the woman he wanted to share everything with, but most of all, he saw the product of a deal.

"Please, just come with me. It won't take long," he tried to convince her.

"You are so cute when you beg," she said and smiled. She pointed a finger at him and said, "You have twenty minutes, no more."

Without hesitation, he got her in his car and drove her to a skyscraper building in downtown Markham. They went to the top of the building, where he had a rooftop dinner arranged, and yet again, it was just the two of them. It was elegantly set up with a red tablecloth, golden utensils, and a beautiful centerpiece of white roses. Soft music echoed overhead. As always, as a gentleman, Alex pulled out her chair and poured her some red wine.

"So what is it you wanted to tell me?" she asked.

Alex took a deep breath and started talking. "I went to a meeting about a job proposition that would make me a lot of money, and the guy I was meeting asked me to do something for him before he would take my deal. He said all you have to do is thirst trap this woman, and he placed a picture on the table. It was a picture of you. I was only supposed to go on one date with you and then report back to him, but the moment I saw you and we spoke, I just couldn't go through with it, so I told him that the deal was off," he explained.

She sat straight up in her chair, frozen in shock, tears pooling in her eyes. She was sick to her stomach from what she was hearing, speechless even.

"Naima, I'm falling in love with you, and I can't see myself with anyone else," Alex said, trying to smooth things over.

A single tear rolled down her cheek as she whispered, "Take me to my car, please."

On the way to her car, he did everything he could to prove to her that he was telling the truth, but she didn't want to hear it. When they got to her car, she got out and didn't say another word to him. She cried the entire way home, thinking how she could have been so stupid, but there was no red flag. *Who would want to do this to me?* She wondered as many thoughts swirled around in her head.

She opened her front door to find her husband preparing dinner, with the lights down low and Teddy Pendergrass's "When Somebody Loves You Back" playing in the background. She could no longer hold back the tears. The tears rushed down her cheeks like a dam had just been broken, converging under her chin then coming to a rest on the neck lining of her dress. She rushed to the bedroom and into the bathroom without the usual affection she and her husband shared whenever they saw each other. Her husband thought that was strange, so he followed her into the bedroom. She locked the bathroom door, so that was as far as he could go.

He stood on the other side of the door and asked, "Honey, is everything OK?"

She didn't want him to know that she was crying, so she took a moment then said, "Yeah, be out in a minute." She took a shower, got herself together, and came out for dinner. Her husband gave her a peck on the lips, and they sat down to eat.

"What was that all about?" he asked.

"I had my menstrual cycle, so I had to rush and take a shower," she replied.

He nodded, and that was the end of that. They finished dinner, watched a movie, and then went to bed.

* * *

Day after day Alex relentlessly tried to talk to Naima and take her out on dates. He even sent her flowers at the office, and as much as she missed him, she resisted and declined his every offer. What she felt for Alex was proving to be too much for her to just forget about him and move on with her life. She would stare off into space and smile as the happy memories of their time spent together danced around in her head. She made a deal of her own with him for them to start over but only as friends, and he gladly accepted it.

They would talk every day, sharing details of how their day went and how much they missed each other. They would make plans for the future with no intention of following through on those plans. It was 9:30 p.m. when her phone buzzed; she picked it up and looked at it, and it was a text from Alex.

"Hi, my gorgeous friend, would it be possible for me to take you away for the weekend?"

She put the phone facedown without replying. She bit her bottom lip as she weighed the offer in her mind. She then turned her head to the right to look at her husband of five years and curled up, sleeping ever so peacefully like a newborn baby sleeping next to his mother. She thought, *I can't do this to him.* Then she turned her head to look at her phone one more time and couldn't help but think about the surreal connection that drew her to Alex in the first place. The chemistry they shared was undeniable, and fighting her feelings had rendered useless.

Her chain of thought was broken by a buzz from her husband's phone. She glanced at it, and it was a text from one of his drinking buddies asking him about how the thirst trapping went. She was stunned with disbelief and disgust, for now she knew who the guy was on the other end of the deal with Alex. Without giving it a second thought, she replied to Alex's text, "I would love to get away."

Alex was elated as he replied back, "I'll make the arrangements."

The next morning, Naima woke up, and her husband was gone, but not before leaving a letter on the nightstand for her.

Naima,

I have made a terrible mistake. I have let my insecurities cloud my judgment, and I have put you in a compromising position when I sent Alex to seduce you. Even though he didn't take the deal, I had to come clean because the guilt is eating me up inside. I hope we can get past it all. I will do whatever it takes to earn your trust again. I know I was wrong and I see that now. I know how much you love me, and you mean the world to me. I just want you to know that. Just tell me what to do and I will do it.

Reading the letter confirmed what she thought she had seen on his phone the night before.

Alex and Naima booked one-way tickets for a very long weekend to the land of love, Paris. There they were in a cedar strip canoe with a single rower at the extreme back. His arm caressed her shoulder as her head rested gently on his. It was as if they were riding off into the orange and pink sunset sky. Meanwhile, her husband sat at home by the window in an old brown recliner, hoping to see Naima's car pulling into the driveway. His and Naima's happiest memories were on repeat in his mind. In his right hand was a bottle of Jack Daniels on the tips of his fingers, on the verge of smashing to the floor, and in his left hand was a letter from Naima.

Dear John,

I have met someone who has shown me more love and affection in the past few weeks than you have shown me in the last five years. I have decided to file for divorce. You will find the divorce papers in the mail as I won't be coming back. Oh, and the man I met, his name is Alex. It seems I would have you to thank for that.
PS Best regards, John.

How he wished he could turn back the hands of time as he read those last words.

Oh, how the tables have turned.

THE END

The Father

Scarlet was drunk yet again. With a pounding headache and blurry vision, she woke up in an unfamiliar place. Searching her pockets and her surroundings unsuccessfully for her phone, Scarlet started to panic. That panic was short-lived when she felt a vibrating sensation coming from her bra. It was her best friend, Nicolette Jamison, calling to check up on her, as she often did. Nicolette and Scarlet grew up in Rose Bay, a beautiful suburb of Sydney, where they were thicker than thieves. You didn't see one without the other. They shared everything; they even shared a boyfriend at one point. Nicolette was smart, reserved, and levelheaded; she always tried to help everyone. Scarlet, on the other hand, was the complete opposite. She was free spirited, very outgoing, and never passed up an opportunity to have a good time.

The girls moved to America the very next day after their twenty-first birthdays. Scarlet had always been drawn to the big cities and bright lights, so they rented an apartment in the heart of downtown San Francisco. Scarlet booked modeling gigs to help with the bills. Nicolette enrolled in college in hopes of becoming a nurse one day, and she also worked the night shift at the hospital most of the time.

Both girls were equally stunning. Scarlet had a thick, full head of wavy red hair that flowed just beneath her shoulder blades.

One look into her piercing hazel eyes and she could captivate your soul. She had a trail of freckles going from one cheekbone over the top her nose and ending on the other cheekbone. Her lips were full, on which she always wore a plum shade lipstick. Her body was long and slender, fitting for the front of *Vogue* magazine. Nicolette was a brunette bombshell; she had a pixie haircut that complemented her straight face. Her body was to die for, and her figure was perfectly proportionate, with curves in all the right places, you might say. So it came as no surprise that they quickly made new friends, and life in the United States became a little bit easier.

The first few months they were living their best lives. They would go out shopping during the day and at night enjoyed the nightlife with their newly found friends—Scarlet and her modeling friends, that is. Nicolette was either attending class, working at the hospital, or working out the math on how to keep up with the mounting bills. Nicolette didn't want to be seen as a Debbie Downer, so she didn't complain when Scarlet came home drunk night after night or when she didn't have her half of the rent month after month; she just did the best she could to support both of them.

One night Scarlet was out with her friends when she got so drunk she couldn't even locate her car, and what did she do? She called the one and only person whom she knew she could count on. "Nic, I need you to come get me," she said, struggling to get her words out.

"Scarlet, I can't come and get you. I'm at work, remember?" she replied with annoyance in her voice.

"Nicolette! I really need your help. I'm at a bar downtown, and I can't find my car."

"What do you mean you can't find your car? Are you drunk?" Nicolette asked as her facial expression shifted from annoyance to anger.

"I'm not drunk. I only had a few drinks. Could you get here already?" Scarlet said while holding herself up against a wall just outside the bar, her red bottom high heels in hand.

Nicolette closed her eyes, took a deep breath, then said, "Give me fifteen minutes. Let me see what I can do."

They hung up, and Nicolette went searching for her supervisor to inform her that she had a family emergency and she would have to leave work to take care of it.

Seeing how much of an outstanding worker Nicolette was, it wasn't particularly a hard decision for her supervisor to make. She had never been late for work, nor had she ever called in sick. She told Nicolette to go home and that she could have the next few days off if she needed more time.

When Nicolette got downtown to the bar, she saw Scarlet sitting on the sidewalk with her legs in the Indian pose position, looking like a homeless yogi. She got out of her car, moved swiftly toward Scarlet, promptly got her into the front seat, and tossed her stilettos in with Scarlet before she was mistaken for a prostitute.

"I have never been so happy to see you!" Scarlet said, talking in an unusually high pitch.

"This has got to stop," Nicolette said sternly.

They got home, and Nicolette dragged her to the bedroom, undressed her of her party attire, and put an oversize T-shirt on her. She then climbed in next to Scarlet, still wearing her scrubs, and they both slept till noon the next day. Nicolette went about the next few days, delicately hinting at the fact that she disapproved of the way Scarlet was behaving lately. She didn't call her out on her bullshit because she knew how overly sensitive Scarlet got when her not-so-proud moments were on display.

* * *

It was a Friday, and everyone was looking forward to the weekend. The city was about to come alive and stay alive for the next two days. Nicolette was simply planning on enjoying her days off by sleeping in and lounging around all day in her pajamas, but at the same time, she couldn't help but think about Scarlet and what she would be getting herself into this time. She got home shortly after nine o'clock in the evening, and as soon as she opened the door, a familiar aroma of tomato basil soup wafted over her. She kicked her shoes off at the door and placed her keys on their hook, which was framed by a picture of her and Scarlet from when they were back home. She paused for a moment, looking at the picture with a reminiscing smile. As she got out of the passageway, she saw an unacquainted but refreshing sight of steam rising from the pots and pans on the stove, heard music blasting, and saw Scarlet dancing back and forth between the stove and the sink with a glass of wine in one hand and a wooden spoon in the other. Nicolette walked up behind Scarlet and tapped her on the shoulder, startling her. Scarlet whipped her body around and slung her arm around Nicolette's neck, squeezing her tightly and at the same time managing not to spill a drop of wine.

"You have got to try this," Scarlet said, shoving the tomato basil soup that sat just on the tip of the wooden spoon in Nicolette's face.

"Hmm, that's good. Is that your mother's recipe?" she asked.

"It sure is," Scarlet replied, smiling proudly.

Nicolette took a quick shower just to wash the long day away; meanwhile, Scarlet finished up dinner and set the table for two. As both girls sat down to eat, they held hands, and Nicolette said grace. "Heavenly Father, we thank you for life and for moments like this."

They both said, "Amen." The girls ate and talked about the day they had.

"It was ridiculous today at the hospital. This guy came in with a nail in the side of his face, and this farmer came in with a huge lump on his back, so they took him to get a biopsy, and there was maggot crawling out of it."

"Gross! You can't talk about that stuff at dinner!" Scarlet shrieked.

"OK, OK. What have you done all day?" she asked, half laughing and chewing a piece of grilled cheese sandwich.

"I had a meeting this morning and a few photo shoots. After that I came back to the apartment."

After dinner, they drank wine and watched reruns of their favorite television shows way into the morning. They slept till late the next day, as was expected, but that didn't bother them because they didn't have anything planed for that Saturday. They just hung around the apartment the rest of the day in their pajamas and had some well-needed girls' time, something they both missed greatly.

* * *

Monday rolled around, and it was back to the old routine. Nicolette started her usual shift at the hospital at 7:00 a.m. sharp, and Scarlet, well, Scarlet was still in bed until around noon, when she slowly made her way to the coffeepot. Nicolette got home around 4:00 p.m., and Scarlet was still in her pajamas. She was surprised to find her at home that time of day, not to mention on a Monday.

"I'm home, and so are you. Are you sick?" Nicolette asked.

"No, I just got up late, and I didn't feel like going to work," she replied.

Nicolette's eyes nearly popped out of her head. "So you just didn't go to work. Do you even still have a job?"

Scarlet didn't reply. She just shrugged and continued scrolling through her phone. They parted ways, which was probably best because Nicolette was boiling at the core. She was running low on tolerance and patience for Scarlet's lack of responsibility; she was getting tired of pulling both of their weights around the house. Scarlet had made promises time and time again about getting better at doing her part when it came to the bills and cleaning up after herself, but those promises had fallen flat. Now Nicolette was questioning her judgments; did she naively made the decision to move away from all she had ever known to come to an unfamiliar country with Scarlet, knowing the characteristics of her best friend? At this point, she was realizing that she was way in over her head, and something needed to change. With everything weighing heavily on Nicolette, she made the very difficult decision to have a sit-down with Scarlet.

"Just hear me out, and try to understand. You know how much I love you and would do anything to make you happy and comfortable, but your recklessness is getting overwhelming for me, and unless you can make a change, I'm going to have to go back home," said Nicolette, laying it all out there for her friend.

"Are you giving me an ultimatum? You wouldn't leave me, would you?" Scarlet asked with puppy dog eyes.

"Call it what you want, but you leave me no choice. I have had it up to here," Nicolette said, with her fingertip just above her eyebrow, indicating her level of frustration.

"You knew how much I wanted to come to America so that we could live life to the fullest," said Scarlet.

"That's beside the point. We can still enjoy life, but at the same time, we have responsibilities." Nicolette tried to explain to her friend, who was acting like a child at the moment.

"Why did you come if you were just going to rain all over my parade?"

"If that's how you feel, I've got just what you need," Nicolette replied, and with that, she left the room.

Their relationship became estranged after that day. They did their own thing for a while, not really caring what the other one did or didn't do.

* * *

After a few weeks have passed and their friendship was still in a less-than-positive state, Scarlet desperately needed her best friend back. With Nicolette's birthday fast approaching, she needed to find a way to make it up to her, and she thought she might have just the way of doing so. Scarlet spent the next week leading up to Nicolette's birthday, planning ways to pull out all the stops. She ordered a very expensive dress straight off the runway and made a reservation at Liholiho Yacht Club. Liholiho was one of the best and hardest restaurants to get into in downtown San Francisco. She hoped that would be enough to win her friend back.

It was finally the big day, and Scarlet was at home, anxiously awaiting her friend's arrival. She heard the door handle turning, so she hurried to the kitchen and grabbed a single strawberry cupcake with vanilla frosting and covered in yellow sprinkles. She lit one pink and blue striped candle, stuck it into the cupcake, and rushed over to the door. The moment Nicolette opened the door, she yelled, "Happy birthday!" shoved the cupcake in her face, and told her to make a wish. Nicolette closed her eyes, made a wish, and then blew the candle out. Scarlet led her by the hand into the bedroom, where she had the yellow dress with black lace trimming around the neck, sleeves, and hem laid out on Nicolette's bed with matching yellow and black stilettos. Nicolette dropped her bags by the foot of her bed, picked up the dress with such force, and hugged Scarlet tightly. Scarlet grinned widely because she was finally making her friend happy. Nicolette pressed the dress up against her body and walked over to the mirror. As she looked into the mirror, she cocked her head to one side, picturing how good the dress would look on her. She ran her hand along the left side of the dress, where she located the price tag, which Scarlet neglected to remove. She looked down and saw that it cost well over a thousand dollars for the dress. Nicolette's happiness quickly turned into sadness. She was like a freight train with steam coming out of her ears.

"How could you afford this dress when you can't even pay your half of the rent?" Nicolette asked.

"I know I have been slacking off on the rent, and I promise to be better, but I really wanted you to have a special birthday, so let's not have this ruin the moment and just go out and have fun," Scarlet replied.

Nicolette closed her eyes, took a calming breath, and said, "You're right. Let's just go out and have fun."

They did just that. They got all dolled up, did each other's hair and makeup, then headed out for the evening. When they got to the location and got out of the car, Nicolette's jaw dropped to the ground in astonishment. She turned to Scarlet and grabbed her by both shoulders, and they both let out a tiny scream. The girls were ushered inside, where their coats were taken right off their backs by a very substantial gentleman. They were then showed to their table, which was covered with a black tablecloth and silver utensils. A low lit candle burned in the center of the table, and a white wine was on chill. The ambiance was welcoming. They were approached by an average-height waiter dressed in all black, with his hair and face well groomed, smelling very manly but in a good way.

He introduced himself as he poured them each a glass of wine, with one hand behind his back. "Hi, I'm Blaine, and I will be catering to your every need for the rest of your stay." He handed them the menu and told them he would be back in a minute.

After he left, the girls looked at each other and said at the same time, "He's cute." They ordered the accidental vegan plate, which was black sesame pita, smoked butter bean spread, crushed brokaw avocado, Jimmy Nardellos peppers, preserved Meyer lemon, cucumbers, pantry pickles, dill, and parsley. They were having the best time they had had together in a long time, but Scarlet wasn't done with the surprise yet. The entire restaurant's staff gathered around and sang a beautiful rendition of happy birthday to Nicolette. As they sang, her eyes filled with joyous tears, and her lips quivered as she tried to keep the tears from leaving her vulnerable eyes. Scarlet, seeing what was unfolding, got out of her seat and made her way to her friend's side. She took Nicolette's head and rested it on her chest. She held her friend as they both listened to the end of the song. They finished their meals and tipped the waiter generously, but that wasn't the only thing they left him. Scarlet wrote her name and number on a napkin, which she then kissed, leaving a stain of red lips. They left the restaurant, collecting their coats on the way out. Even the next day, they still couldn't believe that they had gotten into the Liholiho Yacht Club.

As they were there reminiscing, Scarlet heard her phone ding; it was a text. "Hi, this is Blaine Hartwell. I hope I didn't find you at a bad time. I just wanted to say that you looked amazing last night, and I am looking forward to getting to know you...P.S. Oh, by the way, I hope you left your number for me."

Scarlet jumped off the couch and ran around the living room, and they both screamed.

"Text him back!" Nicolette shouted.

So Scarlet ran to her room, belly flopped onto her bed, and started texting. They made plans to meet up the next day. They hit it off from the get-go. They shared a lot of the same interest, and Nicolette was already breathing a sigh of relief. She was optimistic that Blaine would affect the change in Scarlet that she desperately desired. The two were inseparable, and things were looking promising for their future in the United States until one day Scarlet came through the door grinning from ear to ear. Shopping bags from Gucci, Nike, and Chanel weighed her down on both sides even as she failed to pay her half of the rent once more. Nicolette was infuriated, but like always, she bit her tongue. Scarlet had left her no choice but to do something they both might regret for the rest of their lives.

It was early September, and Nicolette just got home from the grocery store. As she was unpacking the bags, Scarlet walked into the kitchen. She started to help putting stuff away when she came upon a turkey baster.

"What are you doing with a turkey baster? It's not even close to Thanksgiving yet." Scarlet asked.

"It's not for Thanksgiving. It's for you," she replied.

They both busted out laughing, but Nicolette had a more serious look on her face. Nicolette made her favorite pasta, and they invited Blaine over for dinner. It was pasta, friends, and red wine—what could be better? They all enjoyed one another's company so much that they planned to make it a regular thing. It was two weeks later when Blaine showed up for their dinner date. Scarlet had a last-minute photo shoot, so it was just Nicolette at home. She invited him in, and they had a bottle of wine while they waited. After three glasses of wine, Blaine was feeling a little woozy.

"Nicolette, I'm not feeling too good. I think I should go," he said, mumbling his words.

"I don't think you should be driving. I think you should lie down in Scarlet's bed," she suggested. And with that, she took him by the hand and led him to her bedroom. She struggled to get him on the bed.

She then proceeded to take his shoes off and then his pants, but when she started to undo his belt, he slapped his hand on top of hers and asked, fumbling over his words, "What...are... you doing?"

"I'm just trying to make you comfortable," she replied.

"I'm..." He was drifting in and out of consciousness.

She ignored the fact that his body was limp. When he spoke, he wasn't making sense, and he was not at all himself. She got him and herself undressed. She then slipped a condom on Blaine's semi-erected penis, and then she straddled his inert body, slipped his penis inside her, and started rocking back and forth. She derived no pleasure from this anus act, seeing that it was merely a business transaction. When she was finished, she quickly collected the semen in a specimen cup and stored it in a refrigerator, which she kept in her bedroom. Scarlet came home to find Blaine fully dressed and fast asleep in her bed, so she climbed in next to him, and they slept like babies until the next day, unaware of what had just transpired.

Scarlet was still no closer to changing her old habits. Drinking, partying, and shopping were always more important than her responsibilities. One night she came stumbling home, drunk yet again. This time Nicolette definitely had enough. She waited until Scarlet was knocked out, and then she did the unthinkable. Three months later, Scarlet fell ill and had to go to the hospital. They ran numerous tests on her, and that was when they found out she was three weeks pregnant. When the nurse broke the news to her, her eyes rolled back in her head, and her body flopped across the bed she was sitting on as she passed out. When she finally came to, she was screaming and crying hysterically. "Pregnant! How can I be pregnant?"

Blaine gently rubbed her back, trying his best to console her, as Nicolette stood at the foot of the bed watching on with her face guilt-stricken. She was bursting at the seams with this secret she had been holding on to for months now. She bit her lips in hesitation, not sure if this was the right moment to come clean.

But if not now, then when? she thought. As the tension built up in the room, it became impossible for her to hold back any longer, and in a high-pitched voice, she divulged, "It was me...I'm the reason why you are pregnant."

The room went silent. Blaine and Scarlet both looked at her like she was a lunatic.

"Nicolette, I know we are all stressing out right now, but what you are saying makes no sense," Scarlet said.

"I'm sorry, but I didn't know what else to...You weren't taking life seriously, and I was tired of picking up the slack," Nicolette said, rambling and sobbing.

"Nic, please slow down. What are you saying?"

She scrunched her face up in embarrassment and told them how she stole Blaine's semen and implanted them inside Scarlet the night she was knocked out. Scarlet's body was solid like a statue; she just stared at her like a deer in headlights. Silent streams of tears rushed down her cheeks and traveled down her neck as utter disbelief filled her thoughts.

Blaine was mortified at the thought of becoming a dad, but that didn't stop him from reassuring Scarlet that everything was going to be OK. He slowly guided her face by the chin and said, "Hey, look at me. I'm not going anywhere." He then gave her a kiss on the forehead and embraced her tightly.

After a moment, Scarlet stretched a hand out while still in a tight embrace with Blaine, reaching for Nicolette. She shamefully made her way over to both of them and joined in the group hug.

"I love you, Scarlet," she whispered.

"I love you too," Scarlet whispered back.

"I love you both. I mean, you three," Blaine added.

Life is unexpected when you are expecting.

THE END

The Stranger

I'm sitting on a handcrafted wooden window seat fitted with pink soft velvet upholstery, and as I sit in front of this huge window, glass from ceiling to floor, the last of the setting sun peeks in through the branches of an old oak tree, sending rays of light straight at me. Forgetting the rest of the world exists, I find myself drifting in and out of reality, blissfully daydreaming about the moment you first crossed my path. Our eyes met and so did our hearts; it felt like that to me, at least.

It was a Sunday evening, the sun was still out, the air was light and crisp, and so I decided to take my dog, Mellow, for a walk in the park. It was evident that fall was upon us. The trees were beginning to transform, thus dispersing multicolored leaves along the trail. I watched as a flock of geese flew south, with dark clouds at their rears as rain suddenly threatened the blue sky. Before I knew it, big drops of rain furiously made their way to the ground. Drop after drop, I was being hammered in the face hard. I pulled out my umbrella and opened it up, and as I attempted to shelter Mellow and myself, a gush of wind came out of nowhere, knocking the umbrella right from my hand. It rolled down a hill like tumbleweed on steroids, heading straight at a gentleman who had his back turned in our direction. I called out to him, trying to warn him of the imminent collision course my umbrella was on. He unknowingly stopped the roll-away umbrella with his body. So embarrassed, Mellow and I tried to hide behind a tree, but that was an epic fail. He picked up the umbrella, walked over to us, and without looking behind the tree, handed it to me. The rain didn't show any signs of letting up, so I asked him if he would like to share the umbrella and he accepted. I held it up over us and he wrapped his hand around mine to help me hold it in place as the wind was still on a rampage.

His hand was soft and warm, well moisturized, but he had a callus on the side of his left thumb, and for a moment, I was reminded that he wasn't perfect even though he seemed that way, or maybe that was what I wanted—for him to be perfect. His scent was a combination of my wildest dreams and my deepest regrets. His skin was a perfect caramel shade; it looked as if it had been gently kissed by the rising and the setting of the sun. His eyes were the most beautiful hazel eyes I had ever seen. Looking away would be like breaking an once-in-a-lifetime magical connection that once broken, it can never be restored. He was masculine, but I could only imagine his embrace was as kind and tender like that of a mother holding her newborn. He could easily be the crush of both the male and female counterpart. I could feel the warmth of his body as we stood so closely underneath the umbrella, with Mellow looking up at us from between our legs.

I wonder what he thought of me as he stared deep and longingly into my light brown eyes. He was looking at me as though he had something he really wanted to say, and I was looking back like, "Yes, I'm listening," but he didn't pour out his heart, confess his love, or even tell me how beautiful I looked drenched in the rain.

He held his hand up to my face, and before he touched me, he asked, "May I?"

I nodded once, and he proceeded to lightly remove hair that was matted to my face by the rain. His finger brushed against my skin, and my whole body instantly shivered. I felt so light, as though I was in a field of dandelion and I was being hovered aboveground by a cluster of dandelions. There were butterflies dancing in my tummy, and my heart might have skipped a beat or two. Is this what the electricity of connection felt like? I thought he was speaking because his perfectly shaped pink lips were moving, but I couldn't seem to hear what he was saying because I was so deeply immersed in the thoughts of him wrapping one hand around my waist and pulling me slowly toward him until our bodies collided. He snapped his fingers, and I was catapulted back under the umbrella. He waved a hand in front of my face to get my attention.

"Are you OK?" he asked.

"Mmm, uh, yes, I'm fine," I managed to reply.

"Looked like you were lost in your thoughts for a second there," he pointed out.

"Something like that," I replied. If only he knew how lost I really was.

We walked to a flower shop just around the corner, seeking shelter from the rain, but by the time we got there, we were both soaking wet.

"How far do you live from here?" he asked.

"I live maybe a block or two from here. Why?"

"You're wet, I'm wet, and the dog is wet, so I figured I could just walk you home."

I softly bit my bottom lip and then said, "I'm the one with the umbrella, so I think I should be the one walking you home."

He paused as if he was thinking about it, but then he said, "As much as I would like to take you up on that offer, I can't."

"What's stopping you?" I asked with a slightly rejected puzzled look on my face.

"If you take me home, I would have to kidnap you and the dog, and keep you for myself."

As he said that, he tried to keep a straight face, but a faint smile gave his sarcasm away. "I live on the other side of town, so I'll walk you this time, and you walk me the next time," he said.

Thinking there might be a next time, I gladly accepted.

The walk home felt like it took five seconds, but I guess time does go by fast when you are having fun. We talked about pretty much anything and everything we could think of, from what we were watching to our favorite sports, past life, future plans, and liked to do in our free time. We both enjoyed venturing forbidden trail to go hiking, having dessert while watching the sun take a final bow beyond the horizon, and discovering oddly strange songs that nudge just enough at our heartstrings. The conversation was without effort. He held my hand as we sprinted across the street, trying to beat oncoming traffic.

We got to the other side and stopped underneath a tree, laughing at something he said. Out of the corner of my eye, I could see a branch with leaves beading with water, hanging low just over his head. My eyes kept shifting from him to the branch, the branch to him, and I couldn't help myself, so I shook the branch and water went everywhere, which made him scrunch his face up. Oh, he was so cute. I thought it was funny, but then I covered my mouth with one hand, eyes wide open, fearing that he might be upset, but he wasn't. He just returned the favor, shaking a branch over my head. Afterward, he took my face in both hands and wiped away the remainder of water, but when his hands got to the bottom of my chin, he paused, and we both stared in each other's eyes for a lifetime. One bark from Mellow and he was clearing his throat, and I was looking away.

"Yes, uh, you lead the way," he said.

"Right!" I said and started walking gleefully.

He was the perfect stranger, and I was already thinking about when I would see him again. We got to my apartment, and he opened the waist-height swing gate for me. I walked through, and he closed it. Now we were on opposite sides of the gate. He tapped twice on the gate then turned to walk away, but then he paused and looked me in the eyes and said, "See you around, umbrella girl."

It did something unaccustomed to me every time I looked into his eyes. I watched as he ambled back the way we came. His walk told a story. Was it pride? Was it accomplishment? I couldn't quite place it, but it would capture your attention too if you saw it.

He looked back, waved, and said, "I'm Daniel."

I waved back, and before I could say my name, he vanished around the corner. "And I'm Grace," I whispered as my fingers slowly curled inward, and I retracted my wave.

* * *

The following day at work, I found myself in a trance but not just any old trance. Like alternate universe-type stuff, where we are our alter ego, and there are no boundaries to what we can be together. While making a macchiato, I felt him; Daniel walked up behind me and put his chin on my shoulder.

"Hi, gorgeous," he said.

I turned my head to acknowledge him. "Hi, handsome," I replied.

Then suddenly, I heard someone shouting, "You're making a mess! Turn it off!" I was hypnotized by a daydream that felt too real. I couldn't stop myself from thinking about him every waking moment of the day. A song came on and I instantly thought of him. I couldn't understand how one encounter with a stranger had me feeling this way. His face, his smile, his touch, just everything about him caused my face to be laced with a permanent smile. I thought I have a little crush on him, or was it a strong infatuation?

Time and time again, I found myself going back to the place where we first met, in hopes of seeing him, but it seemed like Cupid was on vacation, or better yet, I thought he had retired. I was starting to think that day didn't even happen, it was all in my head, because there was no way he could have felt the way I did, and he still hadn't returned for me on his white horse. *Oh my god, I have officially lost it"* I thought as confusion and embarrassment made their way to the forefront of my face.

In the upcoming days and weeks, I tried my damnedest to go back to my mundane lifestyle, which was going OK until two beautiful ladies came in and sat down at a table in the far left corner of the room. I overheard one telling the other how she bumped into the most amazing guy she had ever met, and that quickly got my attention. I headed over to the table directly behind theirs so I could better hear the rest of this story. I pretended to clean a table so I could eavesdrop, and I heard her talking about his unique walk, his hazel eyes, and his soft hands. Surely she was not talking about...then she said his name— Daniel. I couldn't believe it. I bumped into a chair, and it made the loudest screeching noise as it dragged across the hard floor. They both turned around and looked at me strangely. I quickly apologized and hurried off to the back.

After hearing about this devastating chance encounter between Daniel and a very beautiful woman, I thought I was going to puke. At this point, my thoughts were in overdrive. *Is this the sort of things he did, going around charming ladies and leaving them wanting him? Was I a part of some sick game? How could I be so stupid, or was I just desperate? Maybe this is a different Daniel. You must stop this madness at once.* I encouraged myself.

* * *

Days, weeks, and months passed, and I hadn't seen him again. My umbrella was a constant reminder of the best day of my life, and now all that had been replaced with constant sadness. One morning, as I watered the plants at the entrance of the store, I could have sworn that I saw Daniel jogging on the other side of the street. I yelled his name, but the jogger didn't look back. Were my eyes deceiving me? I needed to see him again; I needed to get closure so I could move on with my life/love life. I turned down dates after dates in hopes of being with the man I fell in love with at first sight. My friends stopped inviting me out because they knew I was just going to cancel at the last minute. My parents tried to visit, but each time I just made up an excuse. Everyone was starting to get worried, calling and texting constantly. I was starting to run out of excuses to tell them. To be frank, I was starting to get worried myself. Out of nowhere his scent would caress my nostrils, but when I turned around, he was nowhere in sight. I was losing sleep. I was not eating like I should. Some days I just stayed in bed, going days without a shower. I looked in the mirror and I didn't even recognize myself; my hair was all matted together. I couldn't remember the last time I washed it. My eyes were as gray as the winter sky; my stomach was hollow to the point of almost touching my spine. Seeing me like that was the jostle I needed to make the very difficult but necessary change.

* * *

The next day, I didn't bother going to work. I called my boss, who was also my cousin, and told him that I would be taking my well-deserved vacation starting now, and the return date was indefinite. I hung up the phone and started packing right away.

As I was looking for clothes to take on my trip for destination unknown, I found some very seductive dress I bought for my dates with Daniel that never saw the light of day, and into the suitcase they went. Who knows, they might get to see the light of day or, better yet, the moonlight even? Not sure when I would return, I packed not too light and not too heavy either, but I thought one bag should do. I called a cab to take me to the train station. I got there at 2:00 p.m., thinking it wouldn't be as busy, but to my surprise, there was a long line at the ticket counter and an old man behind it. The line dragged on and on, people were beginning to get restless. After thirty minutes of standing, moving inch by inch, I finally got to the counter.

"Hi, one ticket, please," I said, looking down in my purse for my credit card.

"Would that be a round-trip or a one-way ticket?" he asked.

My head sprung up, looking puzzled, because I hadn't thought about that part. "I guess…I'll take a one-way ticket, please," I replied.

So he printed the ticket, and as I tried to pay, the card machine stopped working. I started to second-guess myself. *Is this a sign? Is the universe trying to tell me not to go? First, the line took forever, and now I can't pay for my ticket.* I took a deep breath and told myself that I was overthinking it. I tried swiping my card again, and it worked! It worked just in time as the train conductor was doing the final boarding call. I got on and sat down at a window seat. The rumbling of the train engine beneath my seat scared me as the train exited the station and embarked on its journey, and I quickly left my old life and Daniel behind. I would pass a city and tell myself that I would get off at the next stop, but the next stop would come and go, and I would still be sitting in my seat; I just couldn't make myself do it. After twenty minutes and five missed opportunities at a new adventure, the conductor started to check tickets.

When he got to my seat, he smiled and asked, "Hello, little lady. May I have your ticket, please?"

Without hesitation, I handed him my ticket. He scanned it and was about to hand it back to me when he took a second look.

"You were supposed to get off two stops back, so I'm afraid you will have to get off at the next stop," he said apologetically.

My eyes grew large. "But I'm not ready to get off," I said nervously.

"I'm sorry, but I don't make the rules," he apologized again.

I bit down on my bottom lip a little bit too hard, leaving an indentation of my teeth behind, then said, "OK."

As the train came to a screeching halt at the next station, I gripped the handle of my suitcase tightly and whispered, "Time to face the music." I stood by the door, waiting for it open. I could see a crowd of people waiting to board. There were people in suits and teenagers with skateboards in tow. I thought there was even a man of the cloth among them. I dipped my head down and squinted. *I must be seeing a ghost. There is no way that is Daniel,* I thought. I tilted my head back, looked up to the heavens, and asked the universe, "Why are you doing this to me?"

I turned to go back to my seat, but that would prove impossible. I slammed face first into rock solid pectoral muscles. I shifted my eyes upward to find what looked like a dedicated bodybuilder, and he looked a bit annoyed, so I had no choice but to go forward. There was no getting past him. I took one step, and then I missed the last two steps completely. I saw myself face-planting onto the platform, so I closed my eyes, and before I could meet my demise, I felt a pair of hands holding me up. I opened my eyes and thought I had died and gone to heaven. There was a blinding white light at the back of a hypnotically beautiful man; it was hard for me to peel my eyes off him, and so I stared at him uncontrollably. He must be an angel.

"Daniel, what are you doing here?" I asked.

"I'm not Daniel," he replied as he tried to set me upright.

I winced and gave out a hissing sound as I thought I twisted my ankle. "If you are not Daniel...then...who...but you look just..." I tried to caress his face as my words were failing me and so was my body it seemed. I must have passed out because I found myself on a nearby bench in his arms.

"I see you have met my twin sis...I mean, brother," he said.

"If you are not Daniel, then who are you?" I asked, confused.

"I'm David. I hope my brother has been good to such a gorgeous woman," he went on to say.

With anger in my voice, I said, "Your brother is the reason I am on this godforsaken train." Then I proceeded to tell him the whole story.

We sat on the bench and talked, well, I talked for God knows how long, and he just listened. When the story ended, he offered to take me to dinner to make up for what I had been through. I reluctantly declined and told him I must find a hotel before it got any later.

"OK, there's a hotel not too far from here. You should try there first," he informed.

"Thank you," I said and hobbled off. I got to the hotel and asked for their best room.

"I am so very sorry, ma'am, but we are completely booked," said the gentleman at the front desk.

"Could you please check again? I don't have anywhere else to go," I said as desperation overcame me.

"I'm deeply sorry, but if you like, I could call you a cab to take you to the next nearest hotel."

"Sure, thanks." With that, I walked over and sat in an ugly but comfortable chair in the lobby. Ten minutes passed, twenty, thirty, then forty-five, still no cab.

"Welcome back, Mr. Harlow. I have one message here for you."

I looked up from the magazine I was reading, and it was none other than David standing at the counter. I tried to hide behind the magazine, but I was afraid it was too late; he was heading my way.

"What are you doing sitting in the lobby?" he asked.

"Oh, hi! Didn't see you there," I said, playing it cool. "Wait, what are you doing here?"

"I'm staying here. You didn't answer my question," he stated.

"There are no more available rooms, so I'm waiting for my cab," I explained.

"You can stay with me for the night. I have the penthouse suite," he offered. "No funny business, I promise, and you should really put some ice on your ankle," he added.

I looked down, and I no longer had an ankle. "I should, shouldn't I?" So he took me and my bag up to his suite.

When we got to his room, he left my bag at the door, picked me up, and took me straight to the bedroom. He sat me on the bed, propped my foot up with pillows, and placed a homemade ice pack on my ankle. It was ice in a grocery bag from the freezer. We ordered room service and watched movies until we fell asleep.

The next day, I woke up feeling refreshed and optimistic. I was still in my clothes, in the same bed next to David. My arm was draped over his torso and my head on his chest. I opened my eyes to find him gazing at me.

"Good morning, beautiful," he said.

"Where have you been all my life?" I replied and smiled.

The heart doesn't always get what it wants,
but it sometimes gets what it deserves.

THE END

The Blackmailer

Growing up with siblings is typical for any household but not for the Miller family. Out of all the seven Miller kids, James was the only one born different. James was the youngest of the bunch. His physical features weren't impressive, so he got picked on a lot and not only by his siblings. The kids at school saw him as an easy target, and they never passed up the opportunity to give him a shiner. He was five feet six inches of pure skin and bones with curly red hair and a freckled face. He had poor vision, so he wore an oversize round framed glasses. He was the sweetest and smartest kid if you ever got to know him, but he was denied that by everyone, even by his own parents. He would get blamed for everything that went wrong around him, which forced him to retreat into himself.

What happens to a boy who can't find refuge in his own home?

For most of his childhood, James went unnoticed. Keeping his head down, he tried not to get on the wrong side of any-one. But somehow trouble still always found him. When his parents got drunk together, they usually took turns putting out their cigarettes on his arms and legs. During the summertime, temperatures can get up to a hundred degrees in Florida. Kids would be seen running around outside without shirts on, playing with the garden hose. Not James; he was always covered up in long-sleeved shirts and pants, just to avoid the attention his scars would likely bring his way. Certain that he would have gotten teased for wearing that much clothing during the summertime, James locked himself away in his room. He would sit in a corner of his room, with both hands over his ears, trying to muffle the laughter of the other children. At times, he could be seen looking out the attic window, watching on, as boys being boys.

At the tender age of twelve, James felt unwanted; he even got to the point of hopelessness and almost ended it all. With one foot dangling off the small round breakfast table that sat in the center of the kitchen floor, the rope around his neck, and nothing but the tip of his toes keeping him from knocking on heaven's door, he heard a whispering voice, saying, "I need help. Help me, James." He couldn't tell where the voice was coming from, but it was enough to get him down from the table safely. Once down, he tried to locate the source of the voice, but he couldn't. Though he hadn't helped the voice in need, he might have just found his purpose, his way of being relevant. From that day on, he vowed to always do good unto others, and one day someone would notice him for it. That would prove to be more difficult than he had anticipated.

As James got older, he continued to do his anonymous good deeds. One day his car got towed for being parked in a tow-away zone. He had to catch the last bus of the evening that was heading downtown to make it in time for a meeting with his boss. He got to the bus stop just as the bus was pulling away. A passenger saw his attempts to get on board and notified the driver. The kindhearted driver stopped even as passengers complained. He got on and sat in the only available seat, next to a middle-aged man dressed in a gray suit that had seen better days. James said hello to the man, but he didn't reply. He just kept on looking straight ahead. Being a socially awkward person himself, James didn't think anything of it.

James pulled out his newspaper and browsed the headlines. He then stopped abruptly and looked to the passenger next to him, but the man was looking out the window this time. James was sure he heard someone talking to him, but after a quick scan of the bus, he realized that everyone was minding their own business, so he held the paper back up to his face and continued to browse. A few short moments went by, and James heard someone talking to him clear as day. He turned to the man again and asked, "What did you say to me?"

The man looked at him strangely and said, "I didn't say anything to you."

Confused, James stood and started asking everyone on the bus, one person after the other, if they were the one talking to him. Some people looked at him strangely, some shook their heads no, and others just ignored him. Even the bus driver looked at him oddly in the rearview mirror and said, "Sir, please sit down."

Feeling a bit silly, he sat back. This time he heard someone talking but not to him exactly; it sounded like someone was having a conversation with themselves. James listened for a while and wondered if he was going crazy, but then he thought back to the time when he was a young boy, and he heard the voice that saved his life. He couldn't help but wonder if it could be the same voice talking to him again. He tried to ignore it, but the chatter became overwhelming to the point of him covering both ears, shaking his head, and mumbling, "*No, no*, go away!" That didn't deter the voices; they kept calling to him, and one was particularly louder than the rest.

"If I do this, then I might ruin the rest of my life, but if I don't do this, I won't have a life to have the rest of," said the loudest voice.

James looked to the man next to him, not sure if he was the one or what was happening, and shouted out, "What can't you do? Whose life is going to be ruined?"

The man looked at him in disbelief and asked, "What did you just say? How did you know that?"

James, still unsure of what was happening, answered with a question, "Know what?"

"I didn't say that out loud, so how did you know that?" the man asked again.

"But I heard you...in...my...head," James said, puzzled as he placed his pointer finger on the side of his temple. It was at that point James realized that he was hearing other people's thoughts. He wasn't just hearing their thoughts; he was hearing their cry for help. "Sir, I'm not really sure what's happening, but I think I'm supposed to help," he said.

"Help me? I don't need anyone's help, and I most certainly don't need your help."

"But I heard you. That was you, right?"

"Look, I don't know what you are talking about," the man continued denying. At the next stop, the man quickly got off the bus, and so did James. The man noticed James following him and threatened to call the police.

James put both hands up just above his chest and said, "OK, OK, that won't be necessary. Here's my card, just in case you change your mind." He stuck the card into the man's jacket pocket, which sat just over his left pec.

As James got home and got into the house, he started calling out for Jenny to tell her about the man on the bus. He recalled all the events of his day to her and his desperate need to help him, but there was nothing he could do at the moment. He didn't know anything about the man, so now he just had to wait for him to call. That was if he still had the business card James gave him. Jenny then advised him to give it a day or two and then go back to the bus stop where he met the man and see if he would get lucky enough to run into him again. James agreed, but he was also afraid that in a day or two, it might be too late to help him. With that thought, came the sense of helplessness that James knew all too well.

* * *

The next day, James got a phone call from an unknown number.

"Hello. Hi, this is Richard, the man from the bus yesterday."

"Hi, Richard, I'm James, but you already knew that from the card I gave you."

"Let's skip the small talk. Are you sure you can help me?"

"I think I'm supposed to help you, but first you must tell me what you need help with," James said.

"We shouldn't talk about this over the phone. They are probably listening to our conversation as we speak."

"Who is listening?" James asked.

"Meet me tomorrow where we first met, say five-ish?"

The next day, they got on bus 34, the last bus going downtown. "I'm in possession of DNA-altering/genetic mutation codes that, if they fall into the wrong hands, can be catastrophic to the human race. The company that I work for is trying to sell it to the highest bidder without it being fully tested and proven to be safe for use on humans," Richard whispered.

"OK, I see. This is very serious. What is the name of your company so I can do a little more digging? Oh, and give me your number so I can call you when I find something out."

Richard gave James his card, and they both got off the bus at the next stop, and then they went in opposite directions.

James was surprise when he learned that the meeting, he had missed with his boss, was about the very same DNA-altering data. James was now stuck in the middle, with his job on one side and the man he was supposed to help on the other. He went home that day worried and confused about what his next move should be.

"Jenny, I don't know what to do. I want to help Richard, but my boss is counting on me to close the biggest deal of our careers. What do you think I should do?" he asked.

"You should sleep on it and see how you feel in the morning," she advised.

The next day, James wasn't any clearer about who he was going to help. He went into the office with weighted shoulders to tell his boss about the dilemma he was facing. James made his way up two flights of stairs and rounded a corner, and from there he could see his boss in his office through the glass windows. He was on his phone having what looked like a heated conversation. He was making big, aggressive gestures with his hand, and James watched as the color of his boss's face changed, turning from white to red, starting with the tips of his ears. James approached with caution. He opened the door ajar, and his boss tilted his head to the right to make himself visible from behind the screen of his desk computer. He held one finger up, suggesting that James give him a minute to finish up his conversation. James stood just outside the door, and that was when he overheard his boss telling the person on the other end of the phone that he didn't care how he obtained the DNA-altering data, even if that meant taking it off the scientist's dead body, and that he didn't give a rat's ass that DNA wasn't fully tested. He had buyers waiting, and they were the kind of people who didn't like to be kept waiting. He hung up the phone and called for James to enter.

"You needed something?" he asked, with frustration in his voice.

"No, not really, just checking in to see if you still wanted me to reach out to the lawyer, about the former client that is suing us," James asked.

"Yes, do take care of that, please!"

James left the office disgusted and mortified about what he just heard, and he knew what he had to do. There was no way he was going to let his boss get his hands on those files. He called Richard the moment he got out of the building. "We need to meet ASAP. Same spot." He hung up the phone.

They met at the rendezvous spot, and James got right to the point. He warned Richard of the dangers of letting the data get into the wrong hands; James even suggested that he destroy them. Richard got home and pulled out his computer, turned it on, and pulled up the data, and just as he was about to delete the flies, his phone rang. He looked at the caller ID and saw it was James calling, so he quickly answered.

"Hi, James, what's up? I was about to delete the files."

To his surprise, it wasn't James on the other end; it was a woman. Richard moved the phone from his ears to double-check the caller ID, and it was in fact James's number, but it wasn't James's voice.

"Hi, Richard, I'm Jenny. Yes, the files, that's why I'm calling," she said.

"The files...what files are you talking about?" he asked suspiciously.

"You know, the files you and James were talking about."

"Where is James? Put James on the phone."

"There's no need to get James involved. I just want to inform you about the consequences of deleting the files."

"I don't know what you are talking about." Richard continued to deny.

"If anything happens to those files, your death will be made to look like a suicide and—"

Before she could finish that statement, Richard hung up the phone. Not knowing what to think about the whole situation, Richard shut down his computer and had a few more beers than the usual before eventually passing out.

* * *

Richard became so paranoid that he stopped going to work. Every five minutes he peeked in through the closed blinds of his bedroom window and then from the living room window and then from the closed kitchen window. He wanted to call James, but he feared that Jenny might answer. As his anxiety built, he dialed James's number. As the phone rang, he closed his eyes tightly and squeezed the phone in the palm of his hand.

"Hello."

It was James who answered, and Richard finally took a breath. "I don't know what the hell is going on, but we need to meet. I think someone is watching me," he said so urgently.

"Okay, let's meet at the same spot around seven when it gets dark."

It was seven fifteen, and Richard was not at the spot, so James pulled out his phone and called him. He heard a ringing coming from behind him; he turned around to find Richard walking toward him. "What took you so long?" he asked.

"I had to make sure we weren't being followed," Richard replied. "What's going on, James? I thought you weren't going to tell anyone about the files."

"But I didn't."

"Some woman called me from your phone and threatened me that if anything should happen to the files—"

"A woman from my phone, are you sure?"

"Yes, I'm positive. She said her name was Jenny, I believe."

James's eyes grew too large for his face, as if he had just seen a ghost. "I have to go. I'll call you." And he took off in a hurry in the opposite direction where they stood facing, despite Richard calling after him.

Richard put both hands on his head discombobulated as he watched the darkness swallow James. He then headed home, looking over his shoulders at every turn.

James got home, and he was infuriated with Jenny. He couldn't figure out why she would do such a thing.

A neighbor taking her evening stroll heard the screams and glass shattering coming from James's house. As she stopped to get a better look, she saw James in the window, throwing things across the room, and heard a woman repeating over and over that she was sorry. She knocked on the door, and James answered.

"Hey, what's going on in there? Everything OK?" she asked.

"Everything is fine."

"Where's the woman? Is she OK?"

"A woman? Are you sure? There's no woman here. It's just me," James replied.

"I heard a woman crying. I'm going to call the cops."

"I'm sorry. We'll keep it down."

Then the woman left.

* * *

Days went by, and Richard was held up in his apartment and still hadn't heard from James. He attempted to call the police and tell them everything about the DNA, James, Jenny, and the blackmail, but he couldn't bring himself to do it. Instead, he just stayed in his apartment, pacing back and forth, ordering takeout, and praying to hear from James. His phone rang, and he quickly picked it up from the coffee table, flipping it over to reveal the caller ID. Disappointingly, it wasn't James; it was just some telemarketer. He tossed the phone into the side of the couch and let it go unanswered. By this point, paranoia had become him. Meanwhile, James was struggling to find common ground within his own home. On the verge of losing the battle, James finally called Richard.

"Rich! We don't have much time…"

"James! What's going on? I'm freaking losing my mind over here. I think someone is parked outside the apartment. You said you would help me," Richard said frantically, not taking a breath in between his words.

"Richard! Get ahold of yourself and listen to me. You need to get as far away from here as you possibly can. I'll give you a hundred thousand dollars to help you get where you're going."

"A hundred thousand," Richard mimicked silently.

"It would be best if I don't know where you are going, as my mind is not safe," James explained.

"What about the files?"

"Stop right there. The files are never to be mentioned. Guard them with your life."

Then the phone went dead. Richard did exactly what James asked. The very next day, he was on a flight out of the country.

James pulled up to the front entrance of the Internal Self Rehabilitation Center and sat in his car for a moment, reflecting. He then got out and unloaded a single brown leather duffel bag out of the trunk. He walked up to the front desk, and on the sign in sheet, he signed, *James & Jenny Miller*. The secretary looked at the sheet and saw both names, but there was only one person standing in front of her. Confused out of her mind, she paged urgently for the head doctor to come to the lobby. They came and escorted James to the evaluation room. He was deemed a danger to society and was immediately placed on a handful of antipsychotics.

Despite being drugged up all the time, James had still been plagued by the cries for help, but this time it was from all the tormented souls of the facility that had been left without a voice. James spent most of his days in bed with his knees tucked into his chest and his hands over his ears, trying to shield himself from the voices, but that had proven useless. I guess you can say this is what happens to a boy who is forced to rely on himself.

The desire to help others can be overwhelming,
but sometimes one must help one's self first.

THE END

The Betrayal

The kindergarten playground can be a battlefield for any overweight, snotty-nosed kid. Shane Villin was that kid. While most kids looked forward to recess, Shane dreaded the great outdoors with free rein pit bulls for kids. The swings were like death traps on chains; the monkey bars were a no-go zone. The slides were where you would go if you wanted to end it all, so Shane avoided them at all cost. Recess for Shane was typically spent helping his teacher organizing and getting ready for the next lesson. All the energy he didn't expend on the playground was conserved for the after-school one hundred meter dash, when he had to make it to his mom's car in one piece. Shane didn't want to seem weaker than he already was, so complaining about the torture he endured on a daily basis was not an option. He thought if he could just make it through the kindergarten year, then things would get better. Kindergarten came and went, and things only got from bad to worse. Shane was taking a beating at every turn—the boy just couldn't catch a break.

In the hallway of Farmsville Elementary was where Rommel had to come to Shane's aid for the first time at school, after he got slammed to the ground by some older boys. Rommel helped him collect his books up off the floor, dusted him off, and walked him to his class. They got to talking, and Shane finally confessed that this had been going on since kindergarten, and right then and there, a bond was instantly forged. From that day on, Rommel had always had Shane's back. As Shane got older, the more he rebelled and the more trouble he got into. Shane got caught cheating on his benchmark exam and was about to get sent to detention when Rommel claimed it was his cheat sheet and that Shane was taking it away from him. That was the only reason Shane had it in the first place. Rommel got sent to the principal's office, and at the end of the day, he quietly did his time in detention, while Shane got an A on his exam. Their relationship was strange. Rommel didn't see himself simply as Shane's older brother but more of a protector and Shane knew it, so he took advantage of him, but Rommel didn't seem to care too much.

The boys were now in high school. Shane still had all his limbs and his big brother/friend/savior right by his side. They didn't have the same homeroom, so they rarely saw each other at school, and Shane seemed to be doing just fine. He had even made some new friends, friends who reeked of trouble. His elder brother strongly disapproved of them and encouraged him to stay away, but Shane had other things in mind. He finally found a crowd that accepted him—or so he thought—and he wasn't about to give that up for nothing. He went from smoking in the school bathrooms to dealing drugs at the back of the school building. Even though Rommel forbade him from hanging out with his so-called friends, he was still there every time to bail him out of trouble by taking the blame. The principal knew better. He knew that Rommel had nothing to do with such foul acts, but it was his words against Rommel's.

Graduation was around the corner, and Shane wasn't going to be missed by any of the faculty staff. They were going to help him in any way possible to get on that graduation stage and out of the high school. Unfortunately, all their efforts were rendered useless, and they had to suspend him from the school without the possibility of him ever returning. Rommel graduated with a GPA of 4.7 and scholarships from several colleges. He felt guilty for leaving his brother behind, but it was time for him to focus on himself and his dreams.

* * *

Years went by with Rommel reaching out tirelessly to his brother, who seemed to have vanished off the face of the earth. Even though he would have preferred to have his brother in his life, he couldn't dwell on something he had no control over. He had to keep moving forward with life as he knew it. One summer night, the air was warm with a slight breeze, just enough to tickle your face and uncover legs as it blew by. Rommel was hanging out with some of his college buddies at a house party. Everyone was drinking, laughing, and having a good time. There were girls with little to no clothing on and guys without shirts, showing off their athletic physical structure. Rommel walked through the house, greeting partygoers as he went along. With a red plastic cup overflowing with beer in one hand, he fist-pumped people he knew who were close enough to him, and as he navigated his way through the blasting music, carefree dancers, and the alcohol-perfumed air, he pointed to the ones who were out of reach.

He finally got to a spot in the kitchen where he could stand and see his feet beneath him. He leaned against the counter closest to the stove and looked out at the crowd as he sipped his beer with caution. The front door opened, and a group of people walked in. The one who was in front caught his eyes, and he began to stare intensely. As the person got closer, he thought, *It couldn't be.* He was about to take a sip of his beer, but he stopped the cup halfway to his lips. Instead, he looked into the cup, wondering if he was drunk and seeing things. He sat the cup down on the counter and ventured out into the crowd. He got up behind a party attendee and tapped him on his right shoulder. The guy turned around. It had been years, and even though his physical features had changed drastically, there was no mistaking him. His face had a fully mature beard that looked like it belonged on the face of a Greek god, he was way taller, and his body looked like it had been cut straight out of a sport illustrated magazine. Still, Rommel could recognize his little brother, Shane, anywhere. He was no longer an overweight misfit, that's for sure.

"Shane! It's me, Rommel!" he said with such shock and excitement. Rommel pulled his brother in and gave him the tightest hug, almost squeezing the life out of him. Pushing him away from his body while still holding him by both shoulders, he proceeded to examine him from head to toe. He caressed his bearded face aggressively then pulled him in once again for another hug. "Where have you been?"

Shane wasn't expecting to see his brother at the party, so he didn't know what to say, but he didn't need to say anything because Rommel didn't give him a chance to. It was one question after another.

"Why haven't you returned any of my calls? How's Dad? I didn't see you at Mom's funeral."

"Rommel, sorry, I'm not here for a family reunion. You broke the unspoken code between brothers...Brothers never walk out on each other, remember? You left me, and I needed you," Shane said with an icy tone in his voice.

All the guilt Rommel felt on the day he left all came rushing back, hitting him like an eighteen-wheeler going at full speed. "I'm here now," Rommel replied sincerely.

Right as Shane was about to say something, his gaze shifted to the door as a group of young girls walked in. As they stood facing each other, Shane rested his left hand on Rommel's shoulder and said, "I would love to talk more, but I have something to take care of." He then made his way over to the girls, pulled something out of his pocket, and showed it to the well-dressed one who was standing off to the side, looking around. They both walked off to a corner by themselves, and a transaction was made. Shane then reunited with some of the guys he came with.

For about fifteen minutes, Rommel watched on as the party reached its peak. The music was at its highest, but a horrifying scream could still be heard coming from one of the bedrooms. Rommel and some of the other partygoers rushed in to find a girl on the ground, foaming at the mouth. Her eyes rolled back in her head, and her fist clenched as she shook uncontrollably. Rommel noticed that it was the same girl Shane handed something off to not too long ago. Rommel hurried out of the room to find his brother. When he did find him, he was on his way out the front door.

"Hey, what did she take? What did you give her?"

"What did who take?" Shane asked.

"The girl you gave something to earlier."

"I don't know what you are talking about."

"Don't play dumb with me. A girl is in there dying, and I know you gave her something, so what was it?"

"OK, look, man, I gave her some ecstasy, but she took it at her own risk," he said nonchalantly.

"Damn it, Shane!"

Someone must have called 911, as sirens could be heard blaring in the distance. As it got closer, Rommel urged Shane to leave. A minute later, firefighters, paramedics, and cops all showed up. As they rushed the girl off to the hospital, her condition was still unknown.

The next day, it was all over the news. The girl, who was now identified as twenty-year-old Victoria Ellington, daughter of Congressman Bruce Ellington, passed away from an overdose. It was the weekend, so there were no classes in session. Most of the partygoers lay around, nursing hangovers. Rommel instantaneously felt sick upon hearing the news. He made it to the toilet just in time before he puked all over himself. A manhunt was on to find where the pills came from, and Rommel knew it would only be a matter of time before all clues led the police straight to Shane. He did the unthinkable, the most selfless thing you could ever think of. He turned himself in, claiming that he sold her the pills but never meant for any of this to happen. He was arrested and charged with involuntary manslaughter. For his involvement in Victoria's death, he was sentenced to twenty years to life with the possibility of parole after fifteen years.

* * *

The first five years in prison were challenging, to say the least. Shane had only visited his brother once and never so much as a thank you for the sacrifice he made, throwing away his life so that his little brother wouldn't have to grow up behind bars, even though he was about to grow up behind bars himself. Rommel tried to make the best of his life incarcerated.

In the next ten years, he worked diligently to obtain his master's degree in sports medicine, which he couldn't have been more proud of himself for doing. On top of that, he got a letter from his lawyer outlining the terms of parole. Things were finally looking up for him. That was until Shane showed up to see him. He wasn't there for a social visit; he just stopped by to let him know that their father passed away from pancreatic cancer. Rommel was devastatingly hurt to hear of his father's passing, but he must remain focused on his return to free society.

With a degree in hand, Rommel reentered the world after sixteen and half years behind bars for something he didn't do.

Life on the outside took some adjusting to, but he kept a positive attitude. He got a part-time job with a college football team and an apartment in a quiet neighborhood. Life was slowly but surely moving in the right direction. He was feeling a sense of happiness again. Shane was nowhere to be found, but that wasn't anything new. Rommel texted Shane his address and kept him in his thoughts, but he had no hopes of seeing him any time soon.

* * *

Football season came to an end for the team Rommel was working for after their devastating loss. It was another long night for Rommel, so he drove home slowly, unwinding to "Pretty Wings" by Maxwell which he played over and over. He made a right turn into his driveway, and his headlights immediately shone on someone sitting on the second step from the top, with a hoodie on and their head down. Rommel was apprehensive to get out at first, but the person lifted his head, and it was none other than Shane.

"Hey, Shane, it's been awhile. What are you doing here?"

"Hey, Rommel, it's been too long. We should catch up."

Rommel opened the door and let Shane in ahead of him. The brothers drank beer, sat, and talked for a long time.

After that night, Shane kept coming back every now and again. Most of the time, he would come by when he was in trouble and needed a place to lay low for the night or when he got into a fight and needed to be patched up. Rommel was growing tired of his unwanted visits. He warned him not to keep bringing his trouble to his doorstep. One night when Shane was over, the brothers were enjoying a game of pool, which was interrupted when Shane got a phone call.

"I should take this," he said.

"OK, I'll grab us some more beers," Rommel replied.

Shane walked over to the window, with his back facing the room; he looked out the window while talking on his phone. Rommel was about to enter the living room when he overheard Shane telling someone that he was at Rommel's house right now, so he took two steps backward into the passage to further hear the conversation.

"I'm trying to butter him up as we speak so he can go with us to the drop next week. Just in case anything goes down, my brother can take the fall for me. He always does," Shane said.

"Hey, you want another beer or wine?" Rommel called out.

"I'll take a beer," Shane replied, and with that, he ended the call.

They drank and talked some more.

"It's getting late. I should go."

"Hey, you can stay if you want. I've got an extra room."

"Maybe some other time," Shane said.

"OK."

Rommel walked him to the door. Shane got to the bottom of the stairs and turned around as if he forgot something.

"Hey, I've got a business thing coming up soon, and I would love your insight, if you don't mind going with me."

"Sure, send me the details."

"Thanks, brother," Shane said.

The next day, Shane texted Rommel the meetup spot, and he agreed to meet him there. It was the off season, so Rommel had plenty of time on his hands. He did maintenance work around the neighborhood to help out with the bills. While Shane and his guys prepared for the biggest drop they have ever done, Rommel was on a binge-watching marathon of his new favorite show.

The big day was here, and everyone met up at the spot as planned, which was a room at a lavish hotel. They all went up to the third floor at room 305, had their meeting, and made the drop. On the way down, Shane suggested that Rommel go ahead because he and his boys were going to have a drink at the bar in a restaurant at the hotel. Rommel went on without hesitation. Shane wanted Rommel to be the bait, just in case cops were onto them. While Rommel went out the front, they went out the back. As soon as all the men exited the building, they were apprehended by the FBI who was waiting on them.

Rommel decided to do the unthinkable once more. He knew what his brother's plan was, but he went along with it anyways because he had a plan of his own. Rommel wasn't going to let his brother dictate his life anymore knowing he was walking on thin ice being out on parole. He met with FBI agents and told them all he knew. They convinced him to wear a wire, and the ultimate betrayal was committed. Bet Shane didn't see that one coming.

Two can play that game.

THE END

The Spy

Today was rather a very long-drawn-out day. I sat peering out of my window for most of the day, like a cat on a window-sill, listening to music occasionally. The sun sat high in the sky, but there was a chill in the air. It was late spring, but it almost felt like the beginning of fall—the weather was so unpredictable these days. There wasn't much to see; a few cars went by, and one neighbor stood off with a glass of wine in hand, admiring his well-manicured lawn. His grass looked as though he got down on bending knees and trimmed it with scissors. Pride and accomplishment sat on his face as he sipped his wine and nodded in approval.

The middle-aged Irishman, who lived two doors down, across the street from me, hadn't been there in about a week. I had to say this must be the longest he had ever been away. His car was beginning to look like a permanent fixture in his driveway. Its windshield had been redecorated with leaves from the tree branches, which hung a little bit lower than they should, over his fence. The elderly woman who lived next to him was unable to trim the tree; maybe she should get the neighbor with the wineglass to cut it for her with his scissors.

The couple on the right of me argued all the time; I didn't know what time they actually slept. Two, three in the morning they were screaming at the top of their lungs at each other and the dog barking at them to shut up. I wondered what they could be fussing about at that time of the morning, but I tried not to wonder too much; that was uncharted territory. The cops had been called there ten times too many. Nowadays it was like everyone was immune to the crazy that resided in that house, so no one bothered anymore; just let them go at it until someone passed out.

I usually had my groceries delivered to my house because venturing out into the great outdoors with the endless possibilities of what could go wrong was not something I particularly liked to take part in. I had enough crazy here to last me a lifetime. Over the course of the next two weeks, I observed moving trucks going back and forth in the neighborhood. New neighbors, I assumed. Hmm, I wondered what they were going to be like. New people, this meant new data to be collected, my favorite activity. I didn't know, but there was something about the rush of adrenaline I got when my naive neighbors unknowingly made it unbearably easy for me to get in and out of their houses without a trace. I could hardly wait. Who would be first?

Jogging around the neighborhood was a great way to stay in shape, but it was also very useful for obtaining information. There was a young woman who lived two streets over. She couldn't be more than twenty-five years old. She looked athletic, so I was guessing she worked out regularly. She left at the same time every morning, wearing a suit. She drove the newer model of the Genesis, the Genesis GV80 to be exact; corporate job, I was guessing. I hadn't seen her with a boyfriend—or a girlfriend for that matter. What was a beautiful girl like that still doing single? Wait, I was single, ha ha. Maybe I should introduce myself, but what if she didn't go for the computer geek, glasses-wearing type? Oh well, I was sure there were plenty of single women in this neighborhood; I would just have to find them.

On my fourth jog of the day, I observed two Hispanic males loading a suspiciously large rug into a moving van. I didn't want to make any assumptions, but I was almost positive that I heard a moaning sound coming from it. I thought it best to mind my own business, so I didn't bother to trouble the cops with my assumptions. They were going to ask too many questions anyways, and I really didn't have time for that, seeing that I needed to be walking over on Bale Street at approximately six thirty in the evening, so I could see Blondie when she got off work. Like clockwork, there she was pulling into her driveway with her dark green Genesis—that car was a beauty, and so was she. After a few minutes, she got out and unloaded two small paper shopping bags filled with groceries. I like a woman who cares about the planet. She got to the front door and crouched down suddenly, and as I was about to rush to her aid, she popped back up. She removed something from the head of a black-and-white dog figurine. I waited to see what it was, and like I suspected, it was her house key—so predictable.

The anticipation kept me up most of the night. The next morning I jogged to the corner of Bale Street, and as soon as Blondie left for work, I quickly made my way to her front door, making sure no one saw me as I removed the key from the head of the dog and opened the front door. The inside was not what I expected; a warm scent of cinnamon and apple embraced me as I opened the door. I carefully slipped my boot covers on before entering. The layout of her living room looked professionally done, like she paid someone to decorate it for her. She had a lot of family photos on the walls; she seemed like more of a daddy's girl to me. Her kitchen was clean; all the dishes were put away except for a single spoon in the sink. It had some residue on it. I was curious to know what it was, so I picked it up and sniffed it a little; it smelled fruity. Still not sure what it was, I put the tip of my tongue on it, and at that point, I was sure it was peach yogurt. I ran my finger along the counter as I examined the kitchen. Her refrigerator contained eggs, fruits, vegetables, soy milk, bottled water, and two bottles of wine, one half full. Her freezer had more frozen fruits and vegetables; she must be vegetarian or vegan—same difference if you ask me.

I then made my way to her bedroom; the bed was made up with silk bedsheets and pillowcases. I leaned over and smelled her pillow, careful not to disturb anything; it smelled like freshly washed hair. On top of her dresser drawer was a silver platter of jewelry. Every piece of jewelry she owned was laced with expensive diamond, and I should know because I had an eye for that sort of thing. There were watches, earrings, necklaces, rings—you name it, and they had diamonds in it. Her top dresser drawer was filled with a wide variety of lace undergarments; I removed a black one from the very back and stuffed it into my front left jacket pocket. I was sure she wouldn't miss that one. Looking around some more, I noticed a pink silk robe with green feathers on it, hanging on the back of the bathroom door. I got spooked by her cat, so I left, but not before taking some hair from her hairbrush. When I got home, I put the hair and underwear in a ziplock bag labeled Blondie, and then I stored it with the others.

Yesterday morning, I saw a paperboy tossing newspapers in a few yards. I didn't know that Mr. Grumpy read the newspaper, but then again, I was not surprised; he probably would rather read the paper than talk to someone anyways. This morning, I was heading downtown, and it so happened that Blondie and I were heading out at the same time. I was in a car behind her. Oh look, we were even making the same turns, what a coincidence. We got downtown, and she stopped at a bank and went in. She could be doing some banking before she went to work, or maybe she even worked there. If she did work there, daddy must be paying her bills because no bank salary can get you a house and a car like that.

* * *

The Asian couple seemed perfect, but no one is perfect. I was certain that I would find something out of place once I got inside their house. I waited until they were away, and then I sneaked around to the back where I found my entrance—they left a window unlocked just for me. I made my way inside, and once inside, I was always careful not to leave a trace. The inside was what I expected from a typical Asian couple—everything was in its place, and the furniture was free of dust. You could probably see a strand of hair on the floor if there was any. Maybe they were perfect after all. This house was too ho-hum; this was not my kind of fun, and this was a waste of my time.

On my way out the way I came in, out of the corner of my eye, I saw a room with a padlock on it. It was a good thing I had experiences with locked doors, and I never left home without my trusty old lockpicking kit. I meticulously picked the lock, preventing any damage to it. To say I was in complete and utter shock when I saw what was behind that door would have been an understatement. The room was poorly lit with a red light, which was directly pointing to the back of the room, illuminating a wall of dominatrix toys. There was a single bed in the middle of the room. The huge bed had four wooden posts on each corner; the posts had carvings of a dragon wrapped around it from bottom to top. On the bed were two very young, very skinny twin girls, chained up on either end, wearing pristine white lingerie. On the floor next to the bed was what appeared to be hardened candle wax droplets mixed with what looked to me like blood. I had only seen these painful-looking objects on TV, in movies; never would I ever have thought that my innocent-looking neighbors would be the ones possessing them. These people looked like they meditate and pray multiple times throughout the day. The things in that room were barbaric.

I left their house with the highest dose of adrenaline coursing through my veins. Some houses were best left alone, and that was one of them. As I was leaving the Asian couple's house, I saw the paperboy passing by. He wasn't tossing paper, so I was guessing he was done with his delivery for the day and was heading home. He waved at me, so I waved back, trying to avoid any suspicion. He was new around here, so I was sure he didn't suspect anything. I hurried home before anyone else saw me. Nothing for my collection this time, but I was OK with that. I hope the next house would be less intense; never thought I would be saying that.

I had been seeing some police activities lately, a little bit more than we were used to around here; I wondered what that was about. I better be extra careful, wouldn't want to draw any unwanted attention to myself, so I had to be cautious when picking the next house.

* * *

It had been about a week since I ventured into the great unknowns of my neighbors' houses. The rain had been on and off, and plus I had been laying low a bit because of the police presence and all. I didn't know how much longer I could go on like this—I needed my fix. I wanted to feel my heart beating faster than it should from not knowing what I would find when I opened those doors. I wanted sweat beads to slowly form on the palm of my hands as my nerves and adrenaline fought to be in control. It was like the climax at the end of a very steamy, passionate love-making session, with that one person you have always wanted to take you to the heights of orgasm, where you feel like all the molecules in your body are going to explode if they penetrate any deeper or if they put their soft, warm, wet lips on your body. For me, it felt better than that. It was my debauchery.

It took me a while, but I thought I might have found the perfect house to arouse my senses. When I was on one of my daily scouts, I overheard a man on his front porch talking with someone over the phone. I noticed his Russian accent, so I pretended to tie my shoelace to get a better listen. His accent was definitely Russian, but it was more from the southern part that was similar to Ukrainian and central Moscow. I had to do a little bit more recon to get a better idea of when it was completely safe to make my move. The curiosity was killing me! I watched him for about a week, and every Thursday evening at seven, he went to the building where the Alcoholics Anonymous meeting was held, but he never went in. He just stood outside in front of the building until the meeting was finished, and when everyone started to leave, he went across the street and leaned against a tree, smoking a cigarette, watching as people left one by one. The meeting usually lasted about an hour—that should give me plenty of time to get in and out. Next Thursday, that was when I would do it.

* * *

I waited till six thirty, and then I started making my way down the street. At six thirty-five, we made eye contact as he drove past me, going in the opposite direction. I got to his house, and my entry was through the back sliding door. Surprisingly, for someone who smoked, his house didn't smell like it; it just smelled like smoked fish instead. His house wasn't neat and tidy—he had stuff lying around—but it wasn't dirty either; it was somewhere in between. The inside of his house was dark. No family photos except for the one that sat over the fireplace; it was a picture of him, a woman, and a little girl. The little girl couldn't have been more than ten years old. I wondered what happened to them and if that was the reason why he went to the AA meeting.

I looked around a little while longer, but as I went through the rest of the house, it got even darker and more depressing. I entered a bedroom, and on one side of the bed, on the night-stand, was a handgun and a bottle of whiskey, and on the other side, there were woman stuff on a nightstand covered in dust. It looked like they hadn't been touched in years. I was guessing that those stuff belonged to the woman in the photograph, and that must have been his wife. There was a room filled with little girl stuff just lying around, collecting dust as well. After see-ing all that, I had to leave. This house was not my cup of tea. That was my second house in a row that I had to leave without collecting anything.

I already knew where I was going next. Lady Francesca was going to be the one. I went in through the front door like a homeowner would. The moment I opened the door, an aroma of lavender ushered me inside. I closed the door behind me, took my shoes off, and called out, "Honey, I'm home!" I made my way into the very spacious, well-lit kitchen and grabbed an apple from the fruit bowl on the counter. I cleaned the apple on my shirt then bit a chunk out of it. I poured myself a glass of white wine from an already open bottle in the refrigerator, and then I made my way upstairs to draw myself a warm bath. I soaked for about fifteen minutes while I enjoyed the tasty chardonnay.

After the wine was all gone and I was turning into a prune, I stepped out of the tub while it drained and covered myself with a white plush robe, which was hanging on a golden hook on the back of the bathroom door. I used my hand to wipe the steam off the mirror to reveal my handsome face, and I must say that pep-permint bath did me a lot of good. I explored her walk-in closet; all her shoes were color coordinated, and so were her clothes. I started from one end of the closet and ruffled my fingers along her blouse as I walked around in a circle, admiring everything. A bright pink top caught my eyes, so I removed it from its hanger and sniffed it vigorously. It smelled like a mixture of sunshine, freesia, and jasmine. That was a very delightful scent, and I bet that was what Lady Francesca smelled like.

My eyes then fell onto an elegant white dress. It wasn't a wedding dress, but it could have easily been one. The lace and beadwork were exquisite. I ran my fingers over it, one bead at a time, and as I was doing so, I felt a desire, a longing that I had never felt before. I didn't know what came over me, but I quickly returned the dress to its rightful place and went back into the bathroom. I stood in front of the mirror for a lengthy period looking at myself, and who I saw was not the person I wanted to be anymore. It was as if I was snapped back into reality. "I must find a way to change," I told myself as I sat on the edge of her bed. The rush I felt, it kept me alive, in a sense. If I wanted to change, I couldn't keep thinking like that anymore. I wanted a home that was constantly being filled with happy memories, someone to call honey for real, not pretend. As these thoughts filled my mind, I got dressed, I made sure everything was back the way I found them, and then I descended downstairs.

I put my shoes on and opened the front door with a smile on my face, knowing what I had to do next to achieve the life I so desired. There were better days ahead of me; I could feel it. Before I could step one foot out the front door, I heard, "Hands up. Don't move!" My smile was quickly replaced with shock. My eyes looked up in slow motion, and there awaiting my exit were FBI-uniform-wearing hound dogs. At the front of the pack was the paperboy, pointing a gun at my face, and before I could say anything, he was putting cuffs on me. "But...but...you are the paperboy!" I managed to say. He never said a word; his demeanor was very aloof. The next thing I knew, I was in the back of a cop car going down to the station for interrogation.

It turned out that the paperboy was a CIA operative sent to the neighborhood to infiltrate a diamond smuggling ring that Blondie's father operated. I was just icing on the cake, I guessed. I hung my head in disappointment at myself as I found out this revelation. I was about to retire...

The one whom he should have been watching the most was watching him.

THE END

The Dreamer

Vanessa was a single parent raising a child with a very vivid and wild imagination. She would have loved nothing more than to feed her child's imagination, but working two jobs just to provide for both of them, she had no time to spare. With her mom either at work or sleeping, Tila Spearman didn't get to have a childhood that had days filled with fun and enjoyment. She also didn't have a lot of cherishable memories. She spent most of her time with a babysitter, and when she was old enough, she still spent most of her time at home by herself. Traveling the world and immersing herself into whatever culture she stumbled upon had always been a dream for Tila.

Growing up, she was an elaborate dreamer—she would spend hours on end daydreaming about what she would do the moment she became an adult. The list of things she wished to accomplish was extensive and she couldn't wait to get started. At a tender age, she would play pretend. She would often dress up in her khaki shorts, matching shirt and hiking boots, and then she would venture off to the unbeaten path behind her house and into the woods. Sometimes she would be gone for hours without anyone noticing, and when she would return, her pockets would be filled with knickknacks. She had an old brown leather trunk in her bedroom under her bed, where she kept all her finds. Most of what she had were oddly shaped rocks of all sizes and colors. Every once in a while, she would pull out her trunk and admire her collection. As a child with not a lot to call her own, she was very protective of her finds, so whenever she had them out and her mom would enter the room, she would hurry and put them away. Her mom would always ask what that was, and she would quickly change the topic at hand.

Her twenty-first birthday was right around the corner, and her bags were packed and ready to go. Tila and her friend Lizzy booked their tickets, and their first stop was the Forest of Knives in Madagascar then on to the Arashiyama Bamboo forest in Japan. The girls had a lot of traveling ahead of them, and they were beyond excited to get started. The day of the trip was finally here. Vanessa drove the girls to the airport at six in the morning of July 7. When they got to the airport, Vanessa gave both the girls goodbye hugs, but Tila's hug was particularly longer and tighter because she didn't know when she would be seeing her daughter again. The girls threw their arms around each other, and with their other hand, they hauled their suitcases behind them. When they got about thirty feet away, Tila dropped her bags and raced back to give her mom one more hug and kiss for good luck. She jumped into her mom's arms with such force, knocking her back one step.

"OK, go, go. You are going to miss your flight!" Vanessa said as her voice cracked.

"Love you, Mom." And she ran to catch up with Lizzy.

Vanessa blew the girls a kiss then covered her mouth with her hand as tears flowed down her face. The girls vanished into the airport crowd, and just like that, they were off to an adventure-filled life.

The flight was extremely long, but all that was erased once they walked out of the airport, and the warm Madagascar air filled their lungs. The girls stood still for a moment just to soak it all up, and then they caught a cab to the hotel. By the time they got to the hotel, it was nightfall, and even though they were tired, they still took time to admire the magical night sky. It was so remarkably beautiful; it felt like they were on a different planet. They talked about their future plans until they passed out, which didn't took very long to happen. The next day, they were so jet-lagged that they couldn't do the hike, so instead; they hung out with the locals and got a taste of what Madagascar was all about. They even took a crash course on how to speak with a Madagascar accent. The third day, they got the most striking male tour guide that was available, and he walked them through all the safety guidelines before they started their hike. This hike would mark the beginning of the next chapter of their lives, and they were thrilled to get it on the way.

The weather was perfect for a hike; it was only seventy-two degrees. They started their journey on the wooden bridge that stretched over two hundred feet long, with the guide in front of them giving them an earful of the rich history about the Forest of Knives. The girls stopped to take pictures along the way and also to point out some wildlife they spotted below. They were amazed to see animals living among those sharp and jagged rocks, which, in turn, reminded them that nothing in life is impossible. Tila was at the rear as they walked in a line on the bridge to get to the other side. She could feel the gentle breeze at her back, so she released both of her hands from the rope and stretched them out vertically, as if asking the wind to carry her the rest of the way. They were almost on the other side when Lizzy glanced back to check on her and noticed that she looked a little pallid.

"Hey, are you OK?"

"I'm OK. We're almost there. Let's just keep going," she replied.

They got to the end of the bridge, and Tila's knees wobbled beneath her. The guide caught her just before she hit the ground.

"Give her some water. She must be dehydrated," he said.

"One hike down, Japan, here we come," said Lizzy as she held an open bottle of water up to Tila's mouth.

With one trip down, the girls felt like things were heading in the right direction. Japan welcomed them with wide-open arms, validating their decision to go there in first place. The girls didn't waste any time; the very next day, they were on the bamboo trail. The beauty of the scenery was breathtaking beyond words. They both got lost in the serenity of it all. As they went along the path, they brushed their fingertips on the bamboo trees. After finally making it up the hill portion of the hike, Tila turned back around to admire it all. She then made a swift 180-degree turn, bumping into a young English boy, almost knocking the air out of them both. He apologized for not watching where he was going, and she did the same. They looked each other in the eyes and smiled before he awkwardly released her from his grasp, and then they walked away in opposite directions. Lizzy and Tila giggled and whispered as they interlocked arms; onward they went. Tila looked back at the boy at the very moment he looked back at her, and they smiled at each other again.

Later that night, they went for a stroll to see what the local restaurants were cooking up. They saw a little quaint building tucked away in a corner at the end of a street, so they decided to take a peek in the window, and there he was, the same young man from the trail earlier that day. He was sitting at the table by the window; his thick, wavy, shiny dark brown hair lay perfectly on his head. He wore a black leather jacket, looking like a bad biker boy, which was very appealing to Tila. The guy he was sitting across from was not bad on the eyes either. Before the girls could move out of his line of sight, he locked eyes with them. They quickly walked away from the window, but he rushed out of the restaurant and pursued them.

"Hey, you were that girl from the trail," he said when he caught up with them.

"Hi again," they replied bashfully.

"You guys should join my brother and me for dinner."

"That won't be necessary. We don't want to intru—" Tila said, trying to decline the offer gracefully, but Lizzy quickly intercepted her speech.

"We are actually starving, so we would love to eat."

"Great!" he said as he held the door open for them.

The four of them had a night to remember, enjoying one another's company, eating palatable food, and making new connections. The night went so well in fact that Tila and Emmett Crispin made plans to see each other the following day.

The next day, the pair went on their first date. They saw so many places and did so many things. At the end of the day, they sat and watched the water show from a fountain while devouring Yukimi Daifuku, which translates to "balls wrapped into mochi." There was something about Emmett that Tila couldn't get over; she could already see herself making future plans with him in it. His eyes would convey so much excitement when he was with her, and she noticed that, so she was optimistic for their future. They felt like they already knew each other, which made everything that much easier. At twenty-one years old, Tila hadn't had the chance to have someone; she felt like she could have loved from that very first moment they met. When those feelings arose with Emmett, she didn't know how to react to them, but he made it so effortlessly easy she didn't have to know how to deal, other than to just go with it. When they would touch, it felt like everything was amplified. The hair on the back of his neck would stand to attention. She could feel the electricity traveling through her entire body, and she was left feeling his touch for days to come.

The first time they kissed, her body became weightless—there was no gravity holding her to the ground but his gentle arms around her. His voice was like an acoustic guitar made to speak the language of love, being strum by Carlos Santana. They were genuinely happy with each other, and Tila couldn't wait for him to meet her mom. Next, they were off to Paris. Their first stop was the bridge of locks, where they attached a heart-shaped padlock with their names on it, and they kissed the key before tossing it in the Seine River below.

In Greece, they became wedding crashers as they smashed fine china on the streets of Greece, helping a newlywed couple celebrate their new life ahead. When they were done breaking plates, they walked away hand in hand, hands swinging as they went, thinking that it would be their turn one day. They saw snow-capped mountains in Scotland. They shared spontaneous kisses while a blowhole simultaneously erupted behind them. They rode the backs of Arabian camels deep into the Namib Desert in Africa. They explored the unfathomable architectural buildings such as the Copenhagen CopenHill in Denmark, the Interlace apartment complex in Singapore, and a Blobitecture building in Spain.

* * *

Ten o'clock in the evening of July 10, Vanessa frantically rushed to the hospital. When she got to room 114, she stood in the doorway, unable to come to terms with what she was seeing. She clenched her fists as she held herself at the waist, folding forward as she wailed. The head doctor at the hospital walked up in front of her, picked her up, and lay her head on his chest, trying to console her. They then walked into the room together. Vanessa pulled up a chair next to the bed where her daughter lay, with tubes coming out of her mouth. She was in a coma. The doctor explained to her that Tila passed out when she was in Madagascar, and she never woke up.

The doctor stood over her shoulder and watched on as she caressed her daughter's hand with her left hand, and with her right hand, she used Tila's hair to outline her face on both sides.

The doctor stretched forth his hand and hovered it just over her shoulder, but he hesitated, and as he was about to pull his hand back, gravity weighed it down and landed it softly on her left shoulder. She looked up and over her shoulder at him. He was hurting for her, and she could see it in his eyes—at that moment, their hearts both softened for each other.

Vanessa was in that hospital day in and day out to care for her daughter, and so she and the head doctor developed a friendship. He would have a silly joke of the day, every day, for her, trying to cheer her up, and at times it would work, but some days there wasn't anything that anyone could do to alleviate her pain.

One day Dr. Blake stood in the doorway and said, "Hey, beautiful."

Vanessa looked over her shoulder, back at him, and then she pointed at herself in the chest.

"Yes, you," he said as he entered the room. "Would you do me the honor and let me take you to lunch?"

"I would love to, but I can't leave her," she said, looking over at her daughter.

"You can leave her because I'm going to have my best nurse watch over her while we are gone, and we won't be gone that long," he tried to assure her.

"All right, I guess that would be OK."

They went and had a great lunch, and for the first time in months, she wasn't overcome with sadness. They were so preoccupied with each other that they weren't even paying attention to the hours ticking away. Dr. Blake slowly slid his hand across the table to reach for Vanessa's hand, but she quickly pulled her hand away and checked her watch for the time.

"I'm sorry, but I have to go." She gathered her things and left him sitting at the table. When she got back to the room and saw Tila lying lifeless on the bed, she instantly felt a sensation of guilt filling her stomach.

Dr. Blake arrived some time later to apologize for not being more considerate. She accepted his apology but told him that it couldn't happen again. With her emotions naked, he could see how vulnerable she was at that point. Not knowing what to do, he took her in his arms and embraced all of her, and she melted into him. She broke down and let go of all the tears she had been holding back for so long. She then confided in him and told him that she was running out of money, and she wasn't entirely sure how she was going to pay for Tila's stay at the hospital.

"Don't worry. It will work out. It always does," he told her.

Hopelessness is not a good feeling, and Dr. Blake knew that feeling all too well. Five years ago, he watched as his wife of fifteen years expired, because of cervical cancer, so he knew exactly what she was going through. With all the new information at hand, he went before the hospital board the next day to petition on behalf of Vanessa. He then showed up two days later to give Vanessa an update on her daughter's condition.

"She has not improved, but she's not getting worse either," he said, flipping through his papers, checking his notes.

Vanessa was disappointed but hopeful.

"That's not all," he said.

"What is it?" Vanessa asked nervously.

"So I went to the board a few days ago about Tila's stay and—"

"What?" Vanessa asked anxiously.

"And they agreed to let me assume responsibilities of the payments, if you are OK with that?"

Vanessa sat immediately, couldn't believe what she was hearing. "As much as I would be forever grateful, I can't ask that of you."

"You're not asking me. I want to do this, for you." He took both of her hands and looked sympathetically into her eyes as he said that.

Vanessa gave him a sincere hug. He tilted her head up by her chin, and then they shared their first kiss. The two were inseparable from that moment on—well, they kind of didn't have a choice, but they didn't mind seeing each other every day. One thing led to another, and the next thing they knew, they were engaged. Even though they were planning on getting married someday, they were still holding out hope that Tila would be there to see her mom walk down the aisle.

* * *

The years drifted on, seven years to be exact, but little of her visual aspect had altered. Every time Vanessa would look at her, she tried to picture her as the girl she left at the airport that day, vibrant and full of life. Not the girl on the bed, mechanically living. Doctors from all around the world heard about Tila's unusual case and offered to examine her in hopes of figuring out what was wrong with her, but not even the best of the best could offer up a diagnosis. The thoughts of not knowing was eating him up inside, so he worked diligently.

Finally, after sleepless nights, working day in and day out, Dr. Blake got a hunch. He checked deep in her temporal lobe and saw that her hippocampus was somewhat active. He explained to Vanessa that even though she was in a coma, a part of her brain was still active and probably was functioning from the very day she fell into a coma. He then went on to state that the neurological brain waves she was giving off indicate that she was in a dream state. This gave everyone hope that one day she might return to the world of the living.

Once a week, Lizzy would visit her friend and read a chapter or two from her favorite book, *The Adventures of the Lost Girl*. Week after week, Vanessa would bring something from her trunk of finds and place them on the nightstand next to her bed. She wanted her daughter to have a piece of home once she woke up.

Some dreams may never be a reality,
but dream on, Tila, dream on.

THE END

Be on the lookout for Twisted Chronicles Part 2…